S0-ARN-900

RUSTLER'S MOON

K
Hall
&Co.

*Also by L. P. Holmes
in Large Print:*

Brandon's Empire
Flame of Sunset

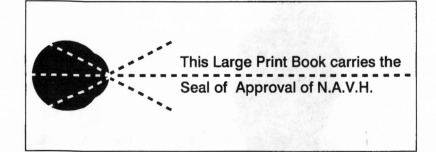

This Large Print Book carries the
Seal of Approval of N.A.V.H.

RUSTLER'S MOON

L. P. Holmes

G.K. Hall & Co. • Thorndike, Maine

Copyright © 1971 by L. P. Holmes

All rights reserved.

Published in 1999 by arrangement with Golden West Literary Agency.

G.K. Hall Large Print Paperback Series.

The text of this Large Print edition is unabridged.
Other aspects of the book may vary from the original edition.

Set in 16 pt. Plantin by Rick Gundberg.

Printed in the United States on permanent paper.

Library of Congress Cataloging in Publication Data

Holmes, L. P. (Llewellyn Perry), 1895–
   Rustler's moon / L. P. Holmes.
    p.   cm.
   ISBN 0-7838-8668-3 (lg. print : sc : alk. paper)
   1. Large type books. I. Title.
   [PS3515.O4448R87 1999]
   813'.52—dc21   99-15674

RUSTLER'S MOON

I

Two miles out of Piegan Junction the Overland whistled its nearing approach, laying out a banner of sound which wrapped around the speeding coaches and spread wailing echoes far across the desert night's great distances. Halfway back in the third coach, Hugh Yeager turned his glance from the rushing darkness beyond the coach window and got to his feet. On the seat beside him were a stout leather satchel and a sacked saddle.

Pausing a moment to time his balance to that of the train's run, he picked up his gear and headed for the vestibule of the car, satchel in one hand, sacked saddle in the other. In the flickering gas lights of the coach he was a high, wide-chested figure in worn denim jeans and jumper. A few travel weary, dozing passengers roused enough to watch this tall, solid-shouldered, brown-faced man fill the aisle with lean, powerful bulk and handle himself with a sure and easy strength as he swung his two items of gear safely over and past their turning heads.

In the vestibule he put down his gear, searched a pipe from a pocket and got it going. With the good smoke of this curling about his face he tried to capture some edge of satisfaction over returning to the home range, but without much success. For that matter, he reflected ruefully, ever since Lorie Anselm's telegram reached him over the railroad wire at the Midland Company's stockyards at Omaha, he'd moved under a depression of spirit so somber it seemed to dry up all the good juices of living. The message had been almost brutally brief.

HUGH:
BUCK ABBOTT DIED LAST NIGHT.
                                 LORIE.

Just five blunt words, though five hundred would not have carried greater impact. And, knowing the sender as he did, Yeager could read the appeal behind that stark brevity. So he closed out the necessary Midland business with all reasonable speed and caught this westbound Overland which presently would put him down beside the cattle pens from which he had loaded an Abbott & Anselm beef herd some three weeks previous.

But that was then and this was now and what awaited him at the home ranch headquarters was anybody's guess. As foreman and riding boss and almost literally Buck Abbott's good right arm while Buck was alive, he'd been a solid and important part of the Double A outfit. Now, in all probability, he was an ex-foreman, as Fletch

Irby would be doing his dirty best to make this a fact. While Lorie Anselm would certainly side with him against Irby, in the end, Yeager knew, it would be Ben Hardisty, the man Lorie was to marry, who would have the final say. And that, unless Hardisty had changed mightily would be nothing more than a soft backdown before Fletch Irby's bull-headed, heavyhanded, aggressiveness.

Again the train's whistle laid its lonely cry across the desert's emptiness. Compressed air hissed and the onward run of hurrying wheels slowed as the brakes took hold. Abruptly from the night the lights of Piegan Junction advanced to meet the train and a porter came to stand beside Yeager.

"Looks like you're the onliest one we drop here, mister."

Nodding, Yeager smiled. "Quick stop for you."

The car lurched as the brakes took firmer hold. The porter lifted the vestibule platform and opened the outer door. The breath of the high desert rushed in, gusty and chill from a great emptiness. The train eased to a creaking halt and Yeager dropped from the steps, boot heels digging into the harsh grit of cinders beside the track.

Up front the bell clanged impatiently and the big Mallet engine blasted hard, staccato exhaust at the star strewn sky. Quickly the train slid away, the brilliance of its headlight a long cone boring into the further emptiness of the night while the parting cry of its whistle thinned to nothingness in the distance. Left only was the reek of coal smoke and oily steam to contend with the strong and familiar pungency of empty, silent cattle pens.

Shouldering his saddle, Yeager cut around the pens and turned up the alley past Duff Tealander's store toward the center of town. Some small reflection of the street lights filtered in at the alley mouth, but mostly here was a thick, layered dark out of which the hostile words struck suddenly.

"It's Yeager, all right. Get him!"

They broke from that dark shadow, three of them, driving and low-crouched. Yeager had time for only one defensive move. He hunched his right shoulder hard forward with a lunge that sent his sacked saddle flying. Forty pounds of honest Visalia rig was in that sack to meet the leader of the three and knock him flat.

Of the following pair, one got by the fallen man, but the other, tripping, slammed into Yeager's legs, cutting them from under him, dropping him heavily into the alley's dust. Then all three were up and at him, one of them swinging a clubbing gun.

Made hurriedly and in the dark, the first chopping blow missed. But the second didn't, and Yeager was saved because it struck glancingly and was cushioned somewhat by the heavy felt of his hat. Even so it hurt him clear to his heels and sent a burst of crazy lights rocketing through his head, leaving him dazed and unresisting for a moment as they swarmed all over him, clawing and mauling.

Bunched, hard-driving knees smashed down on his ribs and a fist hammered the side of his head. The clubbing gun barrel came down again, this time on the point of his shoulder, numbing it enough to let his leather satchel be yanked away from him. The assailant who got it exclaimed.

"Here's the satchel. Let's get out of here!"

It wasn't that easy. Fired with bitter, explosive anger, Yeager came up with a lunge that threw them aside. On his knees, he lifted a warding hand that caught the next swing of the clubbing gun on a spread, grabbing palm. He clamped down on the weapon with grim power and when the owner tried to wrench free, came fully erect. He pushed the muzzle of the gun to one side, twisting his hips to get them out of line and used the drive of this pivoting move to bring his free fist across in a slashing blow that landed solidly.

Now the gun spat, hard report and a pencil of flame, slicing so close it left a burning touch behind. But Yeager still clung to it and again brought his free fist across. This time he felt the cartilage of a man's nose crumple under his driving knuckles. And the gun came free into his grasp as the former owner called a choked warning.

"Watch it — watch it — he's got my gun!"

11

They broke and ran for it then. Just short of the street one of them whirled and scourged the dark alley with two quick, blindly searching shots. A slug ripped a burst of splinters from the side of Tealander's store and the other thudded solidly into something near Yeager's feet.

Yeager reversed the captured gun and with his target now limned sharply against the lights of the street, drove a single careful shot. He saw his target stagger, whirl and drop. Right after, while the echoes still rolled, a pair of horses tore away from the hitch rail in front of Tealander's store and raced out of town.

Yeager went along the alley at a run and was on his knee beside the man he had downed when Duff Tealander, short and broad in his flour-dusted overalls and banker Frank Cornelius, tall and spare, hurried from the store to the edge of the loading platform.

"Who is it — what is it?" called Tealander anxiously.

"Hugh Yeager, and in trouble," was the answer. "Get down here, Duff, and see if you can tell me who this fellow is."

At closer range, Tealander's words were shocked. "He's done for — dead?"

"Yeah, worse luck!" said Yeager, tautly weary. "What a hell of a homecoming . . . !"

"The shooting, Hugh," said Frank Cornelius, "why that?"

Yeager told it briefly. "There were three of them. They jumped me in the alley. They were

12

after my satchel and one of them got it while another tried to gun whip me. When I managed to get the gun away from him, they broke and ran. This one stopped at the alley mouth and tried for me, twice. He had my satchel, so I had to stop him. I wasn't thinking of killing him, just stopping him. It didn't work out that way." Yeager got to his feet and handed the satchel to Cornelius. "Here, Frank — you can take care of it now. The Midland Company payoff for the beef shipment is in there. Right on fifty-five hundred in gold specie."

Along the street men were calling, wondering at the shooting and where it had come from. But only Joe Hazle, town marshal, had the location figured and cared enough to come hurrying. A slender, quiet man, he caught only the last few words of Yeager's explanation, and spoke with quick authority.

"Let's hear it again, Hugh?"

Yeager went over it once more. Joe Hazle listened carefully, then scratched a match and used this brief flicker for a quick survey of the dead man's features. Yeager again spoke his weary regret.

"Complete stranger to me. You ever see him before, Joe?"

"Once," Joe Hazle said. "In the Lucky Seven around the middle of the afternoon today. Him and two others. They were quiet, not bothering anybody. I figured them drifters from the Shoshone Hills, just liquoring up a little before riding on. You say they were after the Midland money?"

"Couldn't have been anything else that I know of. This one had the satchel in one hand and a gun in the other when I dropped him. Never dreamed I'd have to kill a man to get that money home safe. I don't feel too good about it, either."

Joe Hazle shrugged. "What the hell else could you do? Don't let it worry you. This fellow forfeited all rights when he threw down on you. I'll look after things now. You go on about your business."

"Of which he has considerable," Frank Cornelius said. "Lorie Anselm is at the hotel, Hugh. Been there for the past two days, waiting for you to show. But it's best you hear what I have to say before you see her. So come along."

"I got a saddle and a hat back in the alley — both good ones," reminded Yeager.

"Go get them," Cornelius said. "I'll wait for you at the bank."

The acrid breath of powder smoke still hung in the alley. Yeager found his saddle by stumbling over it. He had to use the light of two matches to locate his hat, and when he bent to pick it up the dark world round about whirled uneasily and a fresh surge of misery throbbed in his clubbed head. He probed a gingerly forefinger at the lump forming there and marveled silently.

Luck could sure count for a man — one way or another. . . .

When he returned to the street, Joe Hazle was

14

leaving Tealander's store.

"Duff and me, we lugged that fellow inside for the night," explained the marshal. "And you know something, Hugh — I'm wondering how those drifters come to hear you'd be arriving in town tonight with better than five thousand dollars in your satchel?"

"Now that you mention it," remarked Yeager soberly, "I'll be wondering some myself."

He stacked his saddle on a dark corner of the hotel porch. Across the street things were lively in and about the Lucky Seven bar, men moving in and out as the swinging doors, winnowing back and forth, threw alternate patterns of light and dark. Further along, the bank stood square and solid, a single window glowing yellow.

About to pass the Lucky Seven, Yeager made sudden pause. A man, lank and bony, held the doors of the place half open while tossing a cigar butt into the street. The profile of the gaunt figure was like that of a hunting hawk, hooked and predatory. There was no mistaking it and Yeager murmured his surprise.

"Jack Cardinal! Could it be that with the old herd bull gone, the wolves are beginning to come down out of the hills?"

In answer to Yeager's knock, Frank Cornelius led the way into the bank office. He waved Yeager to a chair and took the one behind the desk for himself.

"The Midland money is in the vault, Hugh, thanks to you. And the gold specie is the way

15

Buck Abbott always liked it. A hard money man Buck was — and a smart one. But he's gone now, and some changes are shaping up for this stretch of country."

"So I noticed," nodded Yeager. "Just saw Jack Cardinal in the Lucky Seven, big as life. Been some time, hasn't it, since he last showed in town?"

"Some," Cornelius admitted. "Joe Hazle is keeping an eye on him, so there'll be no trouble there."

Yeager smiled thinly. "Probably not, seeing there's no cattle in town to steal. Jack Cardinal saves his special talent for the open range."

"And that talent could hang him, some fine day," said Cornelius. "Right now, it's you I'm concerned about. Got any ideas what could be ahead, Hugh?"

Yeager tilted an expressive shoulder. "Only that I'm probably out of a job. Fletch Irby will be licking his lips at this chance to fire me. He's long been wanting to hang my hide up to dry."

"I know," agreed Cornelius. "He's always resented the reliance and trust and authority Buck Abbott placed in you instead of in him. All of which is one big reason why I wanted this talk with you before you met up with either him or Lorie Anselm. As for firing you, friend Fletch is in for a surprise. Now the big question, Hugh. In Double A affairs, how do you rate the importance of the upper ranch — the Sheridan Bench range?"

16

Pondering on this, Yeager searched his pockets for his pipe and came up empty-handed. "Must have lost it during that alley ruckus," he grumbled. "Man gets to depend too much on tobacco."

Cornelius smiled, producing a couple of cigars. "We'll fix that. Try a good smoke for a change."

When his cigar was drawing freely, Yeager spoke with a considered care. "Buck Abbott always said that without the Sheridan Bench range, Double A would only be half an outfit — and not the best half, either. I got to go along with that. Why do you ask?"

"Because," Cornelius said, "that chunk of range is no longer necessarily a part of Double A. It has a new owner, now."

Yeager had been slouched long and loose and weary in his chair. This pronouncement by Cornelius brought him rearing up, stung with amazement.

"A new owner! You mean — while I was away — Buck Abbott sold it?"

The banker shook his head. "Not sold — gave it away. Or, to be more precisely correct — willed it away."

"Willed it — to Fletch Irby?"

"Hell, no! Never to Fletch Irby. Buck wasn't a fool."

"Then to Lorie and Ben Hardisty?"

"No, not to them, either."

Yeager pushed a bewildered hand across his

face. "Be damned, Frank — I don't get this. Who else is there?"

"You, my friend. You!" said Cornelius with open satisfaction.

Yeager stared incredulously. "Me!"

"Just so — you!"

Yeager shook a violent head. "No, no! Man, you're crazy. You don't know what the hell you're saying."

"To the contrary." Frank Cornelius now leaned forward in emphasis. "There's considerable behind it, Hugh. Let's say that among the many things that made Buck Abbott the man he was, he never failed to honor any obligation he felt was fairly his. Such as doing all he could for a dead sister's son, hoping the boy would come up clean strain like his mother. That hope didn't pan out, as in growing up, the boy became his father all over again — and there never lived a meaner, more heavy-handed old bastard than Fletcher Irby, Senior.

"How so fine a woman as Kate Abbott ever came to marry Fletcher Irby, nobody could figure out. But marry him she did, bore him a son; then died early, and was sincerely mourned by all who knew her. On the other hand, when old Fletcher Irby was found out in the sage one day with a bullet through him, more than one responsible citizen poured a quiet drink to celebrate."

"I know," mumbled Yeager. "I know all about that! But the rest — about the upper ranch — the

Sheridan Bench — and me; well, hell, I got to be dreaming. I sure got to because it can't be true!"

"But it is!" rapped Cornelius. "Listen, damn it — and open your mind. Buck Abbott must have known he was about done, because two days before the end he sent for me and Duff Tealander. At Double A headquarters he ran everybody else out of the room, tore up his old will, made us draw up and witness a new one. In it he left the upper ranch — the Sheridan Bench range and all the stock on it as of that day — to you, Hugh Yeager.

"Oh, he didn't cut Fletch Irby off completely, splitting the lower ranch equally between Fletch and Lorie Anselm, the daughter of a one time partner. Neither Lorie nor Fletch know the provisions of the new will and won't until I read it right here in this room tomorrow at ten o'clock. Lorie, I'm sure, will have no objections, but you better get set for fireworks from Fletch. Now that you know, what do you think?"

Yeager shook his head as though still held with disbelief.

"That's the hell of it, Frank — I don't know what to think. Buck didn't owe me anything like that. So why — why?"

Cornelius leaned back, steepling his fingers thoughtfully.

"Duff Tealander and me talked that over on our way back to town. Here's how it shaped up to us. You agree that Buck Abbott felt that whoever controlled the Sheridan Bench range pretty much controlled the future of the Double A outfit. Well, he also thought a great deal of a certain Hugh Yeager, who'd been his strong right arm down through his fading years and he'd come to trust this man Yeager implicitly. Also, when a man has given the good years of his life to the building of an outfit like Double A, when he has toiled and sweated and sacrificed, and on occasion fought and shed good blood for it, then it's natural that he'd want his life's work to endure. It was that way with Buck, and in the showdown he had to choose between you and Fletch Irby to do the job. Had Fletch panned out into the kind of man he'd hoped, Buck naturally would have picked him. But while Duff Tealander and I worked on the will, old Buck told us he saw Fletch as thickheaded, wild and irresponsible and no man to put any real trust in. So the right man for Buck had to be you. There it is, Hugh, the whole picture as I see it — and the only way it makes sense."

Again Yeager pushed a hand across his face, fighting the fog of disbelief.

"You make it sound real enough, Frank. But it will take considerable getting used to. Maybe by tomorrow I'll wake up."

Cornelius chuckled. "You'll wake up, all right. In willing you that upper ranch, Buck Abbott may very well have willed you one hell of a fight. Didn't you just say you saw Jack Cardinal in town? And if I remember rightly there was a time when Mack Snell argued with Buck over the

Sheridan Bench. So far as I know, Snell is still alive and kicking. Finally, there's Fletch Irby. Buck Abbott had his friends, but he also had his enemies, who'll now be your enemies, and for the same reasons. Oh, there's considerable of a chore ahead of you, Hugh. Now, until the word breaks, which it will when I read the will, keep it to yourself while you get on over to the hotel and see Lorie. Buck's death really hit her hard and left her feeling pretty much alone in the ranch picture. She could need a stronger shoulder than Ben Hardisty's to lean on for a time."

II

The hotel was two-storied, the upper half dark just now, the lower warm and friendly with light. Crossing toward it, Hugh Yeager slowed, struck with complete realization of the weight of responsibility Buck Abbott had placed upon him. While it was in effect a legacy of trust and confidence from a man he had greatly admired and respected, it was, as Frank Cornelius had explained it, an obligation implied rather than made explicit in the written word. As of now, the Sheridan Bench range, the upper ranch as it was known, together with all that it held was his to do with as he pleased. But behind that fact lay a proud old man's hope for something his own fading years had not allowed him to fulfill. This, Yeager realized soberly, was an obligation he had to take care of with his heart as well as with his head.

Also, it was hard to shake the feeling of unreality, specific and confident as Frank Cornelius had been. Still, there was nothing unreal about the world out here under the open sky. The night wind, thin and cold, the glitter of the stars and the solid feel of the earth under him made everything stable and good. So he had to believe....

His glance ranged the street. The doors of the Lucky Seven, winnowing again, let out a discord of sound harsh enough to bring Marshal Joe Hazle quickly from the shadows. Plainly the character of Piegan Junction had changed. There was now about the town an atmosphere different than when he had left three weeks ago; a suggestion of latent wildness had taken over. Had this, he wondered, come about because the saddle Buck Abbott had once filled was now empty? Was he, Hugh Yeager, big enough to fill that saddle . . . ?

Frowning over this thought, he climbed the hotel steps and went in. Near the arch leading to the dining room, Andy Stent was fixing the wire bracing of an upended chair. At sight of Yeager he straightened up.

"You're looking for Lorie Anselm; she's in the parlor, Hugh. Helping Helen mend some curtains. Man — what happened to your jeans?"

Yeager stared. "My jeans . . . ?"

"Yeah," Andy Stent pointed. "You try to set yourself on fire?"

Between belt and pocket top and just above the point of his left hip, the fabric of Yeager's Levis was torn and scorched as though a tongue of fire had slashed it. Dropping a hand to cover the spot, Yeager stirred up a sting of discomfort there and he muttered softly.

"I remember it now — the way that slug burned. It was close, Andy — too damn close!"

The hotel owner exclaimed. "Knew I heard

23

shooting! You mean, Hugh, somebody took a shot at you?"

"Somebody did," admitted Yeager wryly. "And the next time you see Joe Hazle, get him to tell you about it."

Inquisitive and garrulous as a jaybird, Andy Stent would, if allowed, stay with an issue of this sort until he'd shredded it down to the last thin detail. But in Yeager there was the urgency of many things to do, so he had shut out further questions by this reply and now moved on into the hotel parlor where Lorie Anselm and Helen Stent were busy with needle and thread, scissors and other sewing equipment.

Lorie had her back to the door, but the sound of Yeager's step brought her around, and with a little cry of greeting she came to meet him. She was a slim, straight, strong-shouldered girl, with a curly crown of coppery hair and a pair of flawlessly clear gray eyes. Made for laughter, her mouth was generous, and the chin beneath, though softly molded, could show plenty of firm decision when occasion demanded. Just now, however, that chin began to wobble a little and tears misted the gray eyes. With no false pretense, she caught hold of Yeager's arms and burrowed her curly head against his shoulder. Her whispered words were choked with feeling.

"If — if I'm acting the baby, Hugh, I can't help it. Ever since I was a very little girl, Buck Abbott was like a second father to me. Always so big and hearty and kind; he held the world steady for me.

Now — now he's gone and I can't get used to it."

"Rough, all right," Yeager said gently. "But knowing Buck, while he'd want us to remember him, he wouldn't want us to mourn too long."

The curly head bobbed in agreement. "I — I know. Just give me a little time."

She drew away presently, dabbing at her eyes with a wisp of handkerchief. Then she squared her shoulders and lifted her head and showed an abrupt change in manner and spirit.

"Now that you're home, Hugh, I want you to promise me one thing. Don't you pay heed to Fletch Irby, no matter what he says."

A thread of amusement quirked Yeager's lips. "Sounds interesting. What's he liable to say?"

"All manner of crazy things. He's already said some of them to me. Hugh, I think I've come to actually hate that man. If that sounds unfeeling, well — it will have to stand. I've tolerated Fletch Irby — at least been reasonably civil to him for old Buck's sake. But no more — not after the way he's begun to act."

Yeager's amusement deepened. "You should get mad more often, Lorie. Becomes you. Makes your eyes turn dark and smoky."

"I'm mad, all right," she declared. "Why Buck Abbott's grave was hardly filled before Fletch Irby started his wild talk about all the things he was going to do. Like taking over the running of the ranch and hiring and firing to suit himself. First of all, he said he'd fire you. Of course I told him I wouldn't stand for that, and that I had as much to say about ranch affairs as he did."

"I'd call that a pretty reasonable statement," Yeager encouraged. "What did he say then?"

"Just laughed in that bullying way of his and said to wait until Buck Abbott's will was read and see how much I had to say. Because he was a blood relation of Buck's, while I was not. Which would make the difference. To prove it, he's already fired Johnny Richert and Miles Grayson."

Yeager's manner sobered. "So—o? Johnny and Miles, eh? How'd that happen?"

"Irby told Frenchy Dubois to throw all your gear out of the bunkhouse, blankets and everything — because you wouldn't be living there any more. Johnny Richert argued with Frenchy about it. So then Fletch took over and when Johnny argued with him he knocked Johnny down and began kicking him around. That's when Miles Grayson stepped in and called Irby off with a gun. So Fletch fired both of them."

"Where'd they go — Johnny and Miles?"

"I don't know," Lorie said forlornly. "I always thought they were two of our best men. But that Fletch Irby . . . !"

"I know — I know," Yeager said. "Well, don't you worry about me and Fletch Irby; I can take care of myself. By the way, I just came from a talk with Frank Cornelius. He said he'd be reading Buck Abbott's will tomorrow morning. I'll see you then, Lorie."

He was about to leave when Helen Stent, silent up to now, spoke with mock sternness.

"You too busy to eat, young man? Won't take long to set up some supper for you."

She was a sturdy, active woman with fine, gentle eyes. Yeager answered her with a grin and lifted hat.

"I'll remind you of that some other time, ma'am."

He got away quickly then, thoughtful as he moved into the street. What Lorie Anselm had told him about Fletch Irby was no surprise. It was about what he had anticipated and a deal he'd face all in good time. Just now it was Miles Grayson and Johnny Richert he wanted to locate. There could be some word of them in the Lucky Seven.

It was still a tower of tumult. Behind his bar, Mike Breedon was a very busy man. In here were some who were sober and some who were not. Looking over the big, smoke-layered room, Yeager saw a number of strange faces before glimpsing in a far back corner a shock of tow hair that could only belong to Johnny Richert. He headed that way, using prying elbows and the swing of his shoulders to work through the crowd. Here he met with several protesting growls, but it was a meeching, nasal drawl that turned him to look into the hooked, vulturine features of Jack Cardinal, who stood near as tall as Yeager but was gaunt and lath-thin. His narrowed, black eyes reflected a sly and mocking challenge.

"I hear," he droned, "that you're out of a job,

Yeager. Could be a lonely ride ahead, wouldn't you say, without Buck Abbott around to back your hand?"

A time or two in the past, Hugh Yeager had had cause to warn Jack Cardinal off Double A range and away from Double A cattle. Now he measured the man briefly.

"I learned to ride alone a long time ago, Cardinal. As for me being out of a job — you can't always believe all that you hear. By the way, how are the back trails in the hill country? Any stray cattle tracks on them?"

He left it that way and moved on, with the slanting, secretive glance of Jack Cardinal following him. In the far corner it was a quick, gusty satisfaction to find Miles Grayson there as well as Johnny Richert. They had a bottle and glasses on the table between them. Yeager pushed the bottle aside.

"Johnny, you're a little too young to drown your sorrows this way. And Miles, you're old enough to know better. Besides, I want sober men working for me."

Miles Grayson came up a little in his chair. He was of middle age, brown and leathery, with squint wrinkles fanning from his eyes' corners. These deepened somewhat as he smiled ruefully.

"Hell, man," he returned, "you're not working yourself. Draw up a chair and help the kid and me empty the bottle. We already got our time from Fletch Irby and you're due to get yours soon as you and him meet."

"Also," put in Johnny Richert, "your blankets and other gear at headquarters are probably laying out in the dirt somewhere."

Johnny had but lately turned twenty-one. He was bareheaded, his hat on the table at his elbow. The lankiness of youth was still in him — he was all arms and legs with a round, boyish face. On his forehead was a bruise and a small cut barely covered by a wild hank of tow hair.

Refusing the invitation to sit, Yeager leaned his spread hands on the table top.

"Just saw Lorie Anselm. She told me about you two. You got your horses in town, of course?"

Miles Grayson nodded. "What about 'em?"

"Go saddle them. You're on your way to the upper ranch on the Bench. Take over there. Anybody who shouldn't comes jingling around — invite them to move on, even if you have to throw a gun."

Now Grayson came all the way out of his chair, a frosty gleam shaping in his eyes.

"I don't savvy why you'd be saying that, Hugh — but, by God, I sure like the sound of it. You wouldn't be jockeying the kid and me?"

"Not at all. You'll hear the rest of it when I see you there tomorrow."

Johnny Richert was quickly up also, flinching a little as he set his hat on his cut head. His glance was eager.

"Might there be another chance for me at Fletch Irby?"

Yeager grinned. "Still full of vinegar, eh? Well, friend Fletch is sure to show. I suggest you leave him to somebody a mite more grown-up than you. He's a little raunchy for a kid to handle."

"Give me a pick handle and room to swing it and I'll cut him down to size," vowed Johnny stoutly. He headed for the door. "Come on, Miles — we're whole men again."

Grayson fell into step with Yeager. "Some wild ones in town since the old man left us, Hugh."

Yeager nodded dryly. "So I noticed."

Coming in, he'd had to elbow his way along. Now, on leaving, the crowd fell back on either side, opening a lane in which Jack Cardinal and a roan-headed follower, one Bruno Orr, stood to bar the way. Cardinal droned a flat statement.

"Little bit ago, Yeager, you made a crack about cattle tracks on the hill trails. It wasn't kindly said or meant, and I didn't take it kindly. Maybe you better withdraw the remark!"

At Yeager's shoulder, Miles Grayson murmured angrily, "The nerve of that damned cow thief . . . !"

"Never mind," Yeager said softly. "I'll handle him. You just keep the rest off my back . . . !"

This was, he realized soberly, something he might have expected. With Buck Abbott in his grave, the power and influence of the Double A outfit was no longer the thing of substance it had been. Nor would it ever be again, unless its role was reestablished. Men who once rode wide of

30

the trail to avoid facing tough old Buck and what he represented were here in this room, prepared to make and take issue. This was a prime example of the change in range politics Frank Cornelius had mentioned earlier in the evening and a challenge that had to be met. Right here and now, Yeager knew, where all present might hear and see, he had to prove something; he had to make a boot track so solid and ruthless it could not be mistaken in outline or purpose. So, coldly and steadily, he looked Jack Cardinal up and down.

"I withdraw nothing. Get out of my way!"

The gaunt outlaw had an extended right arm and hand braced against the bar top like a barrier. But now that arm dropped and swung loose at his sides as he spoke.

"Yeager, you've been entirely too damn proud for too damn long. Bruno and me, we aim to take some of the chestiness out of you!"

Yeager had no gun on him, having turned over to Marshal Joe Hazle the weapon he'd captured in the alley fight. But now the muzzle of a big Colt .44 slid into view beside him, accompanied by a harsh growl from Miles Grayson.

"You try for a sneak, Cardinal — and you're dead. I'll shoot your damned backbone in half. You better believe that . . . !"

The gun and these words caught Cardinal and held him hesitant as Yeager moved in. He caught the outlaw by the slack of his jumper, swung him out and around then heavily back into the bar

31

with bruising, rib-bending impact. From there Yeager sent him staggering into Bruno Orr, where he floundered, shaken and hurt, as Yeager ripped a savage fist into his lank midriff. Caught with his belly muscles flaccid, Cardinal's breath left him in a gasping groan and he sagged down to hands and knees, sick and for the moment, helpless.

Yeager drove on into Bruno Orr, and as it had been with his boss, the unexpected directness and speed of Yeager's attack caught Orr off balance. Before he could recover a sweeping forearm smashed him across the face, tipping his roan head back and leaving his heavy jaw wide open. Yeager hit this wickedly, laying the full weight of his shoulder into the punch. Orr went down in a loose, tangled sprawl, motionless except for a boot toe that drummed twice against the floor before going still.

Came now the rumble of Mike Breedon's big voice along with the thud of metal on wood. The Lucky Seven owner had slammed a sawed-off shotgun on the bar and there was no mistaking his words or the authority behind them.

"Quiet down, everybody! Enough of that. I'm not about to have my place either shot up or busted up. Anybody who wants to argue with a load of buckshot can try his luck!"

"Not here, Mike," declaimed Yeager. "I had to establish my point — now you've established yours." To Jack Cardinal who was hauling himself shakily erect against the bar, Yeager added:

"Where you're concerned, friend — Double A affairs haven't changed at all. Hope I've made that clear. All right, Miles, Johnny, we're leaving."

They went quickly out and lost themselves in the darkness of the night. Miles Grayson's soft laughter came back to Yeager.

"Man, what did you feed on back there at Omaha — tiger meat? Never saw you explode quite that way before. Maybe Johnny and me should send love and kisses to Fletch Irby and tell him to watch his step."

"Not me," chimed Johnny. "I say let Irby find out the hard way."

"Never mind, you two," Yeager grumbled. "What I did, I had to. But not because I enjoyed it particularly. Now get on about your business. I'll see you tomorrow."

They hurried away and presently sounded the mutter of departing hoofs. For himself, Yeager got his saddle off the hotel porch and lugged it down to Pete Piett's wagon yard and stable layout, where he cinched it on the horse he'd left there before leaving for Omaha. Leaving town, he rode in deep, sober thought.

All the events of the night came back to him in vivid detail. What struck hardest was the memory of a man lying dead in the black shadows at the corner of Duff Tealander's store. Good or bad, a dead man was a dead man, and when yours was the hand that had made this so — regardless of justification — left was a depressing aftermath to dull a man's spirit. A thing of this sort was always gone through twice — and the second time around was even harder than the first. Also, he realized gloomily, the way things were shaping up more of the same could lie ahead. Considering what he'd heard from Frank Cornelius and Lorie Anselm, and what he had just left behind in the Lucky Seven barroom, what had begun in conflict must surely end in conflict. Over this he brooded, knowing that however the trail worked out he had to ride it and react as need be to the rough spots as they came along. As old Buck Abbott was wont to say, "Every man had to ride the horse he put his saddle on. . . ."

Accepting this fact, Yeager shrugged aside the depressing thoughts and began savoring the night round about. West the desert ran away, far and flat and formless under the pale light of a gibbous moon. Vague in the east the dark bulk of the Shoshone Hills shouldered up, a barrier against a diminished horizon. But here, when a man rode alone, the desert night and its soothing silences were always good.

Gradually the trace he was riding curbed and slowly climbed and in the deep midnight hour the buildings and corrals of the Double A home headquarters lifted out of the night, dark and silent. Yeager slowed his approach, going in quietly to off-saddle, hang his rig on the saddle pole and turn his mount in at the cavvy corral.

At the open door of the bunkhouse he paused,

once more gauging the night and knowing a sudden weariness. Beyond the bunkhouse door came the sound of sleeping men, a snore or two, the creak of a bunk as a restless sleeper sought a new position. Knowing this building as he did the back of his hand, he went in and reaching for his bunk, found it bare empty of blankets.

The remark Johnny Richert had made in the Lucky Seven came back to Yeager bringing with it a swift gust of anger. Thumbing a match from a shirt pocket he wiped it along the leg of his jeans and lit the kerosene lamp on the bunkhouse table. Sound and lamp glow brought some awakening and two heads lifted. One belonged to grizzled Sam Carlock, the other to Frenchy Dubois. The older puncher exclaimed.

"Hugh! About time. Been hopin' you'd show."

"Just got in from Omaha tonight," Yeager said. "Where's Fletch Irby?"

Carlock shook his grizzled head. "Pulled out around noon. Said something about not being back before tomorrow. He's on the warpath, Hugh."

"Which makes two of us," returned Yeager quietly. He moved along and stood over Frenchy Dubois. "I see my blankets are gone. Maybe you'd know something about that, Frenchy?"

Blinking a pair of black, sleep-blurred eyes, Dubois stared up at him. "Why would I?" he blurted.

"Because I saw Miles Grayson and Johnny

Richert in town and heard what happened out here," Yeager said, bluntly curt. "So you know, all right. Wherever they are, go bring them back here. And everything better be there!"

A sly, half-concealed mockery showed in Frenchy's glance. He snugged back down under his own blankets and yawned.

"Don't know what the hell you're talking about."

Yeager's lips quirked, but it was more grimace than an expression of amusement. Here it is again, he thought, some more of the new opposition, and time to make another boot track in the sand! Ruthlessness surged anew, and his words fell coldly.

"Frenchy, you shouldn't believe all Fletch Irby tells you."

He caught Dubois under the ears and hauled him bodily off his bunk and shook him until his jaw slacked. After which he swung an open hand to the side of the head that snapped like a breaking board, whirled Dubois around and dropped him back on his bunk.

"Now, God damn you — pull on your boots and go get my gear," Yeager ordered harshly. "If I have to work you over again to make you understand I promise you there'll be no fun in it!"

Frenchy Dubois's glance was weasel red, his face twisted into snarling lines as he went out, weaving a little. From a wall peg above his bunk, Sam Carlock slipped a holstered gun free and tossed it to Yeager.

36

"Keep your eyes open, Hugh!"

Out in the cold, early morning dark, Frenchy Dubois mouthed a spasm of silent, murderous cursing to ease some of the fury convulsing him. But in the end, he decided venomously, there'd be time enough to take care of Yeager when Fletch Irby returned. So, from the shed floor where he'd thrown them earlier, he collected Yeager's blankets and war-bag and carried them back into the bunkhouse. The blankets were tangled and dust-smeared.

"Shake them out good and make up my bunk," Yeager told him relentlessly.

Dubois showed another burning glance but did as he was told. Yeager returned Sam Carlock's gun and got his own from his war-bag. The weapon had not been tampered with nor were any of the other contents of his war-bag missing.

"At least," he told Frenchy Dubois cuttingly, "you stopped short of being a complete damn thief!"

Even as he spoke, however, one more dismal certainty came to him. To handle what now lay ahead, the mere weight of his fists would not be nearly enough. From now on he'd have to live with this gun . . . !

III

The Sheridan Bench was a far-running shelf of country tucked into the massive flank of the Shoshone Hills. It stood a full fifteen hundred feet above the desert floor and when feed became short on the lower range during the late months, there were still lush meadows and open parks scattered among the stands of timber on the Bench. Every summer, over the years, Buck Abbott had moved beef cattle up from the desert to this high range to fatten for fall shipment. It had been his ace in the hole and he had held it tenaciously against all challenge.

Switching back and forth, a road climbed the long slope from the desert and mindful of the directions Hugh Yeager had given them, Miles Grayson and Johnny Richert kept their mounts steadily to the road's dragging slant. Round about, the night lay vastly still and empty and when they finally moved on to the first level reach of the Bench, the world was chill under the light of the stars and a sickle moon that hung low in the west. Johnny Richert unwrapped a coat from behind his saddle cantle and shrugged into it.

"What you figure Hugh's up to, Miles?"

"We'll find out tomorrow," Grayson said. "Until then I'm satisfied to still have a job and a sound roof to spread my blankets under."

The Sheridan Bench headquarters had started originally as a small and spartan-bare line camp, but when Buck Abbott, to escape the desert heat during the hot months, took to spending more and more time up here, he'd built for greater comfort and permanency. Now the headquarters of sturdy logs lay long and low, with two wings angling out from one big central room. One wing consisted of kitchen and bunkroom, other of two bedrooms, one for Buck Abbott, the other for Lorie Anselm's use whenever she had cause to stay overnight.

The large central room had a table and several chairs scattered before a big fireplace. A floor to ceiling closet filled one corner of the room and there were numerous wall pegs to hang things on. A massive set of elk antlers hung over the fireplace and a gun rack against a wall held a couple of Winchesters and an old, but still potent Sharps buffalo rifle Buck Abbott had used in his younger days. Several partially empty boxes of ammunition for all three rifles were stacked on the wide stone mantel of the fireplace. A kerosene lamp stood on the table.

The horses put up for the night in a feed shed behind the ranch house, Miles Grayson lit the lamp and led the way to the bunkroom. He put down the lamp and began pulling off his boots.

"I'll sleep better not having that Frenchy Dubois hombre around. He's just too damned slippery to suit me."

"How about Fletch Irby?" Johnny offered.

Grayson stretched and yawned and put out the light. "Two of a kind," he said.

Young and healthy, Johnny Richert was quickly and soundly asleep until some time after midnight. Then he wakened to a combination of gunfire and drunken yells that brought him lunging from his blankets in bewildered alarm. Across the room Miles Grayson was growling a steady wrath.

"Come alive, kid — come alive! Hugh warned us — and now we're caught like this. Get into your boots and come on. But keep out of line of the door . . . !"

Grayson led the way with Johnny stumbling at his heels. "Mind what I said about the door," Grayson warned again. "The walls will stop anything they're throwin' but the door won't . . . !"

Johnny had heard of affairs like this in the early days, but here, for the first time in his young life, he was under actual gunfire. A strange mixture of fear and a heady excitement gripped him. Gun reports outside were a heavy thudding, as though muffled by the dark. Bullets pounded into log walls and stopped there, but others ripped and slashed through the splintering door into the rear wall of the room. Shattered window glass smashed on the floor. Here was the real danger, these slugs that found entrance. Any one of them would lay a man dead on the floor. . . .

"Over here, kid — over here!" Miles Grayson urged.

Johnny made it and had one of the racked Winchesters shoved into his hands.

"Load this thing, find yourself a window and give them hell," Grayson told him. "And hold low — low! You might get lucky."

Johnny did his best, swinging his rifle, spacing his shots. It was blind shooting as the sickle moon had gone down and the early morning dark had turned thick as velvet. At another window, still growling that steady wrath, Miles Grayson was searching the dark with his own vengeful fire.

Outside the attack wavered and began to slacken. "Keep after 'em, keep after 'em, kid!" encouraged Grayson. "They don't like their own medicine. I'm going out there . . . !"

The shattered door slammed open and Grayson was through it, crouched and running for the protective corner of the kitchen wing. Safely sheltered there he dropped to one knee and cut down on the flash of an attacker's gun, levering three quick shots in reply. A man yelled — yelled again — and then there was a rush of departing hoofs and night's heavy silence returned.

Miles Grayson waited out a long pause, then prowled the dark before presently returning to the house.

"Lost their salt quick when the lead started

coming their way," he announced triumphantly. "Just a bunch of damn drunken yellow-bottomed coyotes. You all right, kid?"

"A little shaky," Johnny admitted truthfully, "but figure I'll make it. Who do you think they were, Miles, and why would they want to shoot up the place?"

"Buck Abbott is dead and buried, yet they were still shootin' at him. These hills are full of such scum that old Buck chased back into the brush at one time or another in the past. Even though he's dead and gone, there's nothing they'd like better than take a bite out of Double A. We could be seeing a lot of such from now on. Well, how's for stirring up some breakfast? You can smell the dawn outside, so there's no point in going back to bed."

From odds and ends of kitchen supplies, Johnny put together a passable meal. By the time they finished eating, the first gray light of day was seeping across the Bench. They went out for a look around but found nothing more than some empty rifle shells at the edge of the clearing. These weren't enough for Miles Grayson. He saddled up his horse.

"I'm interested in where they came from and where they went. There should be plenty of trail sign. You stick around, kid. Keep that Winchester handy and don't let anybody sneak up on you. From what he told us, Hugh Yeager will be along later on. If I'm not back by that time, you can tell him what happened."

At a few minutes past nine in the morning, Fletcher Irby rode into Piegan Junction. He hauled up at the Lucky Seven hitch rail, but did not immediately dismount. Instead he made a slow survey of town, up street and down. In the saddle he was a blocky shape, thick through chest and shoulders, with heavy thighs that stretched the legs of his jeans to tight capacity. Slightly swarthy, his features were set with a sullen arrogance and his eyes, brown and hard, were as unrevealing as murky bottle glass.

Mike Breedon, cleaning up after a day and night of heavy trade, bustled out of the Lucky Seven door behind a busy broom, pushing the accumulated debris ahead of him. Spur chains clashing as his boots met the ground, Irby left his saddle, throwing a blunt question.

"See Hugh Yeager around, Mike?"

Breedon shook his head. "Not this morning. But I saw a lot of him last night. So did Jack Cardinal and Bruno Orr. Likewise, so I understand, some stranger who tried to get away with the beef payoff Hugh brought in from Omaha. Overall, I'd say certain people who might have figured Double A had gone soft because Buck Abbott wasn't around any longer got one hell of a surprise. Because Hugh Yeager proved it hadn't!"

"He's no part of Double A now," Irby countered irritably. "I'm doing the hiring and firing for that outfit. And Yeager's one hand I can do without."

Mike Breedon leaned on his broom, his glance narrowed, speculative. He shrugged and turned, pausing in the saloon doorway.

"Now I'd think on that, Fletch — was I you. I really would. Because Hugh Yeager is a damned good man. Also and besides, maybe he won't fire easy . . . !"

The saloon doors winnowed behind Breedon's disappearing figure. Irby scowled, took another look at the street, then unbuckled his spurs and hung them on his saddle horn. He crossed to the hotel moving with his thrusting, slightly pigeon-toed walk. On the hotel porch he seemed to put extra weight into each stride as if to draw attention by the hard, echoing impact of his boot heels. At the register desk, Andy Stent was hunched over a Winnemucca newspaper. He looked up and nodded.

"Mornin', Fletch!"

Irby grunted, then added: "Too late to scrape up some breakfast?"

"Not sure. Lorie Anselm and Ben Hardisty are having coffee. Could be some left in the pot. You should have been in town last night, Fletch. Hugh Yeager sure stood certain people on their ears."

Irby grunted again and went on into the dining room. At a table near the kitchen door, Lorie Anselm and Ben Hardisty were having coffee and a platter of hot cakes. Waiting no invitation,

44

Irby hauled up a chair to the same table. He grinned sourly at the quick, protesting turn of Lorie Anselm's auburn head.

"Sure I'm buttin' in," he said heavily. "But I can't wait for a better time to tell you both how things are going to be out at Double A from now on."

"We've been over all that before," returned Lorie tartly. "No amount of further talk will change my stand one bit."

Irby shrugged his thick shoulders. "Then I won't bother with you. I'll do my talking to Hardisty here. Maybe he'll show better sense than you do."

Ben Hardisty was a sober, quiet, mild-mannered sort, a year or two past thirty. He ran a small spread just off the west side of the Double A desert holdings. He looked at Irby and spoke with his usual mildness.

"Lorie's mind is her own, Fletch. So are her opinions. I found that out long ago. So anything you might say to me won't change them."

Irby hunched forward, his big, meaty hands on the table edge. "I don't know when you two figure to tie the knot, and I don't care. But one thing I'm damn sure of, Hardisty. If you think by marrying Lorie Anselm you'll have anything to say about Double A affairs, you couldn't be more wrong. Because I'm running Double A now — I am! There'll be no three bosses, or two of them, either. Just one boss — me! Now if you've got that fact straight, we'll go on with the rest."

45

Helen Stent came out of the kitchen and looked at Irby with no great pleasure.

"Way past breakfast time," she announced flatly.

Irby indicated Lorie and Ben Hardisty. "They're eatin', ain't they? Well, I'll be satisfied with some of the same."

Helen Stent's attitude did not change. By every visible sign she had no use for this man, Fletcher Irby. But she also saw that the making of an unpleasantness lay ready and waiting here, so she nodded briefly.

"Very well — I'll feed you."

The heavy-featured grin Fletch Irby sent after her held a triumphant mockery as he turned back to Lorie and Hardisty. "See how it is," he gloated. "You tell them off, you get action. Now here's the rest of it for you two. I'll buy out Lorie's interest in Double A and then . . ."

"Buy me out!" Lorie cut in. "What with? You haven't any part of that kind of money. Besides, I'm not interested in selling."

"You will be," Irby taunted. "And I'll have the money. Soon as Abbott's will is read, I'll have the money. So you better listen and turn sensible; things will work out easier all around."

Lorie got to her feet. "I'm not listening to another word. Come on, Ben!"

Hardisty moved to push away from the table, then hesitated. "Let's not jump the fence, Lorie. Fletch may have something worthwhile to offer. Won't hurt to listen."

Lorie's eyes were flashing as she looked down at him. "I said I would not listen — and I won't!"

She wheeled away then and went into Helen Stent's kitchen. Fletch Irby's laugh was short, eruptive, guttural.

"Ben, somewhere along the line you'll have to take a whip to that woman of yours. Buck Abbott spoiled her to death. She needs to be eared down plenty!"

"We're not talking about that," Hardisty said curtly. "If you got a proposition, let's hear it. But see that it makes sense."

Irby laughed again, as though enjoying some joke of his own. "It'll make sense, all right. But don't you and the girl figure to use the spurs on me. Get your heads together, work out a fair figure for her share and we'll do business. But get this once and for all. I'm the boss at Double A and what I say goes. If Lorie Anselm or anybody else sets out to stand in my way, they'll get run over. The same goes for you. So get about your figuring and let me know."

At a quarter of ten, Hugh Yeager came into town, his horse at an easy canter. He tied at Tealander's rail and went in. Duff Tealander was at the rear of the store, checking merchandise.

"Hope you're not bringing any trouble with you this time, Hugh," he greeted.

"That's a good thought, Duff," Yeager agreed. "Now I want you to put up a buckboard load of grub supplies for Pete Piett to haul out to the upper ranch on Sheridan Bench. Also, if you see Joe Hazle before I do, tell him I'm paying all and any costs coming from last night's affair in the alley. I see it as my responsibility."

Duff Tealander studied him for a moment, then nodded as though confirming a previously formed opinion. "More and more I realize Buck Abbott made no mistake in the things that count." He indicated the gun slung at Yeager's hip. "Been some time since I last saw you carrying one that way. You figure things warrant it?"

"Afraid so," nodded Yeager soberly. "Which reminds me. Throw in half a dozen boxes of .44s with the grub order. Put it all on the books. I'll be around some time later to settle up."

"I'll have Pete on the road inside an hour," Tealander promised.

Back in the street, Yeager squared his shoulders in the sunlight and went along to the bank, noting that town was considerably quieter than last night. He turned in at the bank, heard voices in the office and went there. Besides Frank Cornelius, three people were present. Lorie Anselm, Ben Hardisty, and Fletcher Irby. At sight of Yeager, Irby reared heavily to his feet, blurting: "What the hell is this, Cornelius? What's he doing here?"

"Answering my summons," was the curt, vigorous reply. "For a reason you'll soon find out."

"I see this as strictly Double A business," argued Irby. "And Yeager's no longer any part of the outfit. Right here and now he stands fired!"

"Something aside from my business," retorted the banker brusquely. "For the moment I want to get at an obligation left me by a dead man, and I intend doing it in my own way. So if you want to hear what Buck Abbott's last will and testament has to say quiet down and listen. Otherwise, get out!"

Fletch Irby subsided, glowering. Taking a chair, Yeager met Lorie Anselm's glance and the small smile of relief it revealed. He nodded and smiled back.

Standing tall and straight behind his desk, Frank Cornelius spread a paper before him and spoke with a quiet emphasis.

"The wording of this will is as blunt and direct as was Buck Abbott himself. There is no windy phraseology involved. It means what it says, and says it simply and quickly.

"To Lorie Anselm, daughter of my long dead partner, Dean Anselm, I leave one full half of my lower ranch, including range, cattle, riding stock and all other necessary equipment. To Fletcher Irby, son of my dead sister, I leave the other half of the lower ranch, together with range, cattle, riding stock and equipment.

"My upper ranch, the Sheridan Bench ranch, in its present entirety of range, cattle, riding stock and necessary equipment, for past invaluable and faithful service, I bequeath to my good friend and trusted foreman, Hugh Yeager."

"What's that — what's that?" The words came

out of Fletch Irby explosively as he again surged to his feet. "Cornelius, you're lying! I know what Buck Abbott's will said. I know what . . . !"

He broke off abruptly. Frank Cornelius had opened a desk drawer and from it lifted a stubby barreled, but heavy caliber Bulldog six-shooter and laid it on the desk, ready to his hand. The glance he showed Fletch Irby was bleak as polar ice.

"Irby, the only reason you're staying to hear the balance of this is so you can not claim any misunderstanding at some later date. Furthermore, I take not another damn word of blackguarding from you, understand! You throw the lie at me again, I'll drive it back through your teeth with a slug. Now — sit down!"

Fletch Irby dropped back, the swarthiness of his face congested with angry blood. His head swung from side to side, like that of a surly bear, eyes red and smoldering with baffled feeling. Frank Cornelius cleared his throat and read off the balance of the will.

"All current funds on hand and in the vault of my trusted friend and banker, Frank Cornelius, shall be divided equally three ways between Lorie Anselm, Hugh Yeager and Fletcher Irby to use at their own discretion."

The banker's head came up. "That's it," he said. "This will is properly signed by Buckley Abbott and properly witnessed by Duff Tealander and myself. It is valid, explicit and will stand against any challenge." He laid these

50

last words directly in Fletch Irby's lap. And for Irby's further benefit, added: "You may have known — or thought you did — what the conditions were in Buck Abbott's old will. But two days before he died, he sent for Duff Tealander and me and in our presence destroyed that old will and drew up a new one, this one." He tapped it with a forefinger. "He had his own reasons for doing it. Are there any questions?"

"Yeah," growled Irby savagely. "Just who in hell talked the old fool into making this change?"

"Nothing influenced him except his own good sense," retorted Cornelius. "It was his own decision entirely, arrived at not because he was a fool, but was instead a very wise and very fair man. I now lock this document in my vault."

Cornelius walked out. Again Fletcher Irby lurched to his feet, putting his angry glare and growl on Hugh Yeager. "All right, Yeager, all right! So he gave it to you. Now let's see if you can keep it!"

"Well I aim to, Fletch," Yeager assured him dryly. "I sure aim to."

Irby stamped out, burly and threatening.

Yeager turned to Lorie Anselm. "It's your opinion I worry about, Lorie. What do you think about my part in this?"

"I think it is very fair," was the quiet reply. "I know how completely Uncle Buck depended on you during his last years, and how completely you lived up to his trust. You deserve what he left you, and I'm glad, Hugh. Because, in a way,

51

you're still part of Double A, which makes me feel safer about my part."

Returning to the office, Frank Cornelius had a flicker of a smile for Yeager.

"Some explosion, Hugh. But not as bad as we expected."

Yeager shrugged wryly. "Could come later," he prophesied. "Well, finding myself the surprised owner of a working ranch, I better get out and start taking care of it."

"You'll be needing money," reminded Cornelius. "Remember, there's a fair chunk of it waiting for you."

"Get to that later on," Yeager said. Caught by a thought, he turned back to Lorie Anselm. "Anywhere, any time you need help of any kind — let me know."

Silent up to now, Ben Hardisty spoke with a sudden sharpness. "I think that's my chore, Hugh — taking care of Lorie's affairs. You agree?"

Marking the startling heat in Hardisty's glance and manner, Yeager nodded.

"Just so you do a job of it, Ben. Good luck!"

Stepping into the street, he saw Pete Piett heading out of town with a loaded buckboard. He got his horse and followed.

In the bank office, Ben Hardisty faced Frank Cornelius.

"A little more information could have considerable effect on the plans Lorie and I have for the future. Any objection to telling what a third of the cash money Buck Abbott left amounts to?"

Frank Cornelius showed him a brief, still, very direct glance before tipping a shoulder.

"Not at all. Understand, Buck Abbott never coveted money just for money's sake. A fair balance of ready cash on hand for any real emergency satisfied him. The rest he poured back into the ranch and the things he figured constituted real value — range and grass and cattle. I haven't had time to make a final, complete check in the matter, but at a rough guess I'd say there was somewhere around thirty thousand, give or take a few hundred. Which means that Lorie's share is about ten thousand." The banker's glance went to her. "What do you want done with it, Lorie?"

"Right now, leave it as is. Uncle Buck made the ranch pay its way. There's no reason why my share shouldn't continue to do so."

Cornelius nodded. "Smart girl."

Lorie moved toward the door, but Ben Hardisty lingered for still another question.

"In the event Lorie should decide to sell her share, what would you consider a fair asking price?"

Lorie came quickly around, the flags of impatient color whipping her cheeks. "Ben, I'm not going to sell. I told you that."

She marched out, shoulders very straight as she headed across the street toward the hotel. Ben Hardisty had to hurry to catch up with her.

"Do you have to act this way?" he demanded,

showing a touch of anger himself. "I'm only concerned with what would be best for our future."

"So am I," Lorie retorted. "But Uncle Buck didn't leave me what he did to have me turn right around and sell it. If you're still thinking of what Fletch Irby offered, just forget it. Because even if I ever did sell, it would never be to him."

There was a streak of persistent stubbornness in Ben Hardisty that kept him arguing.

"Lorie, you're not using your head. So you've no use for Fletch Irby. Well, neither have I. Which is the whole point of my argument. How long do you think we could operate out of the same headquarters with that man? How long do you think we could stand his damn rawhide and bluster? Buck Abbott split the lower ranch even up between you and Irby. Now tell me — where does your half of everything start and where does his half leave off?"

He plodded on, head bent, staring down at the street's tawny dust.

"Be different if it was somebody we could get along with. Somebody who wouldn't try to be whole hog and run everything. But Fletch Irby would never meet you even up and leave it so. You know that. With him it would be battle and misery all the way. That's it — battle and misery. And in the end everything would go to hell, ranch included. Can't you see how that deal would be?"

Some of the defiant straightness went out of Lorie's shoulders. She half turned and dropped a placating hand on Hardisty's arm.

"I don't mean to be contrary, Ben. I know how hopeless is the chance to get along with Fletch Irby. Just the same, I can't bear the thought of selling to him — no matter how much he was able to offer. To someone else in time, maybe — but never to him. Right now, I don't want to sell to anybody. No matter how things work out, that is how I feel."

"You can't stand balky on a creek bank forever," declared Ben Hardisty, logically enough. "The water ain't about to dry up before your eyes. You want to cross that creek, you got to get your feet wet. Somewhere along the line you got to make up your mind, one way or the other."

"I know, I know," Lorie admitted, a little wearily. "But I want to think on things for awhile."

IV

Climbing the switchback road from the desert flats to the Sheridan Bench, Hugh Yeager was in no great hurry. Up ahead some hundred yards, Pete Piett kept his buckboard team steadily to the pull and Yeager was content to have it so and hold his place. In fact, he preferred it this way, for he had to get used to the enormity of change in his personal fortunes, and it wasn't something that came easy.

Many times in the past he had made this ride when the climb had been merely a tiresome stretch to put behind him. Today, however, things were different. Today, every step his horse took carried him just that much closer to something that was his — his! It was a feeling that grew steadily and when the road finally topped out and leveled through meadows and open parks where white-faced cattle stopped in their feeding to stare, he savored the realization of possession so strongly, it became an emotion that left him fiercely exultant yet strangely humble.

Up ahead the buckboard slowed abruptly and shrill complaint lifted. Yeager closed in quickly as Pete Piett continued to lay out his startled wrath.

"Now just what's the goddamn idea — throwin' a gun on a man and scarin' he'll out of him? Duff Tealander told me to haul this grub up here for Hugh Yeager. Which is all I'm doin', so why you meetin' me with a gun . . . ?"

"Sorry, Pete," said young Johnny Richert. "Just making a little bit sure of everything." He stepped from a timber stand into the road with a rifle across his arm. "Didn't mean to give you a start, but after last night, Miles Grayson and me — we ain't taking any chances."

Pete Piett was short, rotund and choleric. He waved a stubby arm. "I dunno nothin' about your troubles, but havin' the muzzle of a gun stare me in the eye allus did scare the tall bejasus out of me. Can I go along now?"

"Sure — sure!" Johnny moved aside and waited for Hugh Yeager, who made curt inquiry.

"What about last night, kid?"

Johnny told it soberly. "Miles and me, we came straight here from town like you ordered. Everything was quiet, so we turned in to get some sleep. Little past midnight somebody started yelling and shooting up the place. Soon as we could get organized, we spread some lead of our own. This discouraged them outside and they cleared off. But there's fixing to do. The ranch house door is shot full of holes and some of the windows are knocked out."

"Any idea who the raiders were?" Yeager asked.

Johnny shook a troubled head. "That's where Miles is now, out trying to locate some trail sign and see where it leads. We were caught plumb off guard, Hugh, and we're no ways proud about that."

Yeager shrugged it aside. "So long as neither of you stopped a slug, the rest doesn't amount to much. Where's your horse?"

"Back in the timber."

"Get it and come on."

A hundred yards beyond and some two hundred north of the ranch house, a timber-furred canyon slanted down from the higher reaches of the Shoshone Hills. A little stream of cold, clear water splashed from the canyon mouth, curved past headquarters, gurgled under a short log bridge and some half mile further down the range lost itself in a small lake in an aspen swamp.

Pete Piett's buckboard rumbled across the bridge and hauled up before the ranch house. Pete got out of the rig, took a sack of flour across his shoulder and started to enter, then stopped to stare. Built of heavy, sawn pine planks, the door was pocked and splintered with a scatter of bullet holes. The fat little livery stable owner exclaimed.

"Would you look at it, now! Who'd want to shoot up a man's door like that?"

"I might make a fair guess, Pete," Yeager observed. "Some day I'll likely know for sure."

"Since old Buck left us the country shows

58

signs of goin' bad," Piett grumbled. "Me, I ain't what you call a fire-eater, but should somebody shoot my door full of holes, I'd be mighty tempted to shoot back."

"Not a bad idea," Yeager concurred.

Johnny Richert rode up and the three of them unloaded the buckboard. Then, as Pete Piett headed back for town, Yeager made his survey of the night raid's damage. Moving from room to room the slow, cold anger mounted and fumed again. Not that the allover damage was great, which it wasn't. But what there was of it represented a senseless vandalism or drunken destruction to arouse any solid man. Somehow, to shoot up a man's home was to express a certain contempt for its owner.

"How many would you say were in the gang, kid?"

"Maybe half a dozen from the way the shooting sounded. And kind of like they were liquored up and figured they were shooting up an empty layout. They discouraged quick when they found it wasn't." Marking the increasing harshness of Yeager's expression, Johnny added: "We'll be doing something more about it?"

Yeager's nod was definite. "First, we'll wait for Miles."

It was past midday when Miles Grayson rode in. His report was terse. "They cut south from here to the Massacre Pass Road, then over the pass and down into the Elkhorn Flat country. So I figure it was likely Jack Cardinal and some of his crowd, out to get even for the rawhidin' Jack got in the Lucky Seven."

"Just so," agreed Yeager. "Elkhorn Flat is Cardinal's favorite country."

"Him and others," Grayson said. "Last time I was through that way, Mack Snell was holding down a chair on the porch of that deadfall Gabe Norton runs." Grayson showed Johnny Richert a hard grin. "Either you or I got lucky last night, kid. There's a dead bronc half a mile this side the pass road, and somebody or something leaked gore all the way over the summit. So we didn't waste all the lead we threw."

"The brand on that dead bronc tell you anything?" Yeager asked.

Grayson shook his head. "One of those crazy Paiute brands. Only an Injun or God Himself could read it. Man — do I smell coffee cooking?"

Johnny Richert had put a meal together, and as they ate Yeager laid out the picture of the new state of affairs. Both riders were startled and exultant.

"Smart man, Buck Abbott — always was!" exclaimed Grayson. "This still kinda keeps the old outfit together. Also, puts that knucklehead, Fletch Irby, in his place."

"Won't keep him there," Yeager warned. "Last thing Fletch said to me was 'So he left it to you. Now see if you can keep it!' "

Johnny Richert had his head cocked as he listened intently. "Somebody riding in." He went to a shot out window for a look. "It's Lorie

Anselm and Sam Carlock. Old Sam looks kinda the worse for wear!"

Yeager was quickly outside to greet the arrivals. A time or two before he'd seen Lorie Anselm really angry, so he did not miss the signs now. Spots of color burned in her cheeks and her eyes were smoky dark with emotion. Her shoulders were combatively stiff as she came quickly from her saddle and over by Sam Carlock's horse, ready to lend its rider a hand.

Sam Carlock looked like he could use some assistance. His lips were cut and all one side of his face was swollen and livid with bruise. A shaking weakness racked him, and he sat hunched low on his horse as though there was pain in his body.

"Sam, what is this?" Yeager asked. "Who did this to you?"

"Try one guess," came the thick answer. "You won't miss very far."

"Fletch Irby?"

"Part. Mostly Frenchy Dubois."

Sam Carlock had been the oldest hand in point of years and length of service in the Double A outfit. A man in his middle sixties, he was gaunt, grizzled and kindly, and frankly past his prime in point of usefulness. But as an old-time crony of Buck Abbott's, he'd been sure of a home at Double A while Abbott lived.

"Because of last night, Sam?" Yeager asked, recalling how the old fellow had tossed him a gun while warning him against Frenchy Dubois.

"Dunno," mumbled Sam. "But maybe. Don't

matter. Just one thing for sure. They ever come at me again, I kill Irby and Dubois. I'm too old a man to take any more pushin' around by that pair." He pressed a hand against his side and hunched lower in his saddle.

They lifted him down and got him inside to a bunk. Shrewd and observant, Miles Grayson spoke up. "Johnny and me, we'll look after Sam. Maybe, Miss Lorie — you got things to tell Hugh?"

"Yes," was the swift answer. "I have."

In the big center room she faced Yeager. "Can he stay here with you, Hugh? Where he'll be safe?"

"As long as he wants," Yeager said. "Now — how'd this come about?"

She couldn't stay still. She paced the room, clenching and unclenching her hands, trying to ease the emotion seething in her.

"That Fletch Irby!" she burst out. "I can't stand being around him any longer. And I don't know what to do about it. But I won't sell to him — I won't . . . !"

Yeager took her by the arm, eased her into a chair.

"What's this about selling to him? First mention I've heard of it."

She explained the approach Irby had made in the hotel at breakfast, and how she had told him flatly that she wasn't interested in selling, least of all to him. "And then," she added, "when Ben and me rode home after the meeting with Frank

Cornelius, Irby was there ahead of us and right away he began it again, demanding I set a figure I'd take for my share of the ranch. When I insisted again I wasn't interested in selling, he started to threaten and get abusive. Old Sam heard him and came over to protest. Irby knocked him down and told Frenchy Dubois to run him off the place, that Sam wasn't riding for Double A any longer. Dubois wasn't very gentle about following Irby's orders. He seemed to enjoy kicking Sam around."

"And you say," reminded Yeager bleakly, "that Ben Hardisty rode home with you? He was there while this thing went on?"

There was a degree of cruelty in the question, and it wasn't easy to answer. Lorie became still in her chair, her head lowered. Slowly she nodded and her reply came muffled.

"Yes, he was there."

"What did he do about it? What did he have to say?"

The lowered head dipped lower still. "Noth . . . nothing much. He did try to calm Irby down, saying that after I'd thought it over maybe I'd listen to a fair offer. Ben's been in favor of me selling right from the first, if Irby's offer was enough. But — but . . . !"

"I see." Yeager said it gently. This was a proud girl he stood beside, and he could sense and understand the shame she was feeling. "But of course, you don't want to sell . . . ?"

The auburn head lifted once more and shook

violently. "No — and never, never to Fletch Irby!"

"Then don't you," Yeager said. "For that matter, I don't know where Fletch Irby would figure to get enough money to meet a fair price for your share. I see I'll have to have a talk with Fletch. A real, down-to-earth understanding that's been long overdue."

Lorie looked up at him. "And you'd take my part, of course, as you always have. But it's not fair that you should shoulder my troubles along with your own. Just so you take care of old Sam is all I ask, Hugh."

"He's exactly the man I want, and he's working for me," Yeager told her. "Someone to stick close to these headquarters, handle a few small chores and do the cooking. As for Fletch Irby, he's bound to be my trouble as well as yours. One thing is very certain, you can't stay alone at the desert ranch with the way this thing is shaping up."

"Where else would I stay? Somebody has to keep an eye on my share of the ranch."

"My chore," Yeager said. "And you stay in town with Helen Stent."

She would have protested this, but he shut her off. "Few weeks ago I was bossing both lower and upper ranches. No reason why I can't again. Now I head for town. You're going with me."

She faced him, gravely murmuring, "Why is it I always lean on you when I'm in trouble?"

He showed a small grin. "I'm built to carry weight, like a broad-backed horse."

The town of Piegan Junction dozed lethargically in late afternoon heat when Yeager and Lorie Anselm pulled up at the hotel hitch rail. Lorie left her saddle reluctantly.

"I still feel guilty, Hugh. Promise you won't get into trouble with Fletch Irby on my account."

"I'll just let him know that I'm watching to see you don't get shortchanged somewhere along the trail," Yeager assured her. "Suppose you promise me something. No matter what — you won't sell!"

"No matter what, I won't."

"Good girl! Now to locate Soddy Neff."

He tramped off down the street. On the hotel steps, Lorie looked after him soberly. She entered the hotel slowly and in deep thought, as though seeking an answer to some vital personal question.

Yeager found his man behind a shop bench littered with fragrant sugar pine shavings. Soddy Neff was a spidery, sharp-featured person who could perform sheer wizardry with a saw and a hammer and a wood chisel. With him now in his shop, passing an idle half hour in casual talk, was Town Marshal Joe Hazle.

After brief explanation of the why of them, Yeager gave out his list of needs. "You'll have to replace some windows and build an entire new door, Soddy. You'll take care of it?"

"I'll ride out and measure for the door," Soddy nodded. "Big rush for it?"

"Seeing that it has to be done, maybe the sooner the better."

"Tackle it first thing in the morning," promised Soddy. "That's pretty raw stuff, Hugh, shooting up a man's house. Once they figure the bars are down, some people can turn real rough."

When Yeager moved to leave, Joe Hazle fell into step with him.

"Add 'em up, Hugh. Last night's affair in the alley, and the fuss afterwards in the Lucky Seven. Now they shoot up your ranch house. My friend, somebody is gunning for your hide!"

"Just so," Yeager agreed. "And the hell of it is, I'm no trouble hunter. I'd have no quarrel with any man, if they'd just leave me alone."

"Ah!" exclaimed the marshal, "that's just it. But they won't." He tapped the badge on his shirt. "One way or another, one place or another, I've packed one of these for a lot of years, so I recognize the signs and know what comes of them. In the rhythm of life and death, men move in and out of the picture. Some of them, like Buck Abbott, throw a shadow high and wide enough to keep other men in line. But once that shadow fades, look out! Then the wolves start howling at the moon. That's the way it always goes, Hugh. And it always spells trouble!"

Yeager's head bobbed in somber agreement.

"If there's an answer, Joe — and you know it — tell me."

"The answer is, you do one of two things. Either you quit and run, which means you'll keep running for the rest of your life, or you do what Buck Abbott did. You take the gloves off and build a tall shadow of your own. Whatever you have to do — you do! If it means throwing a gun, you throw it, and for keeps. If it means using your fists on a man, you put weight behind them. You try and stay inside the law, but you don't back up one thin damn inch. You might, in time, tame a four-legged wolf with kindness, but you never will one of the two-legged kind. You try it with one of them, he'll figure you weak and go for your throat.

"Now from what Frank Cornelius has told me about Buck Abbott's will, you've become an important man along this range. Which could make you an important target for some people. Buck Abbott was just such a target in the early days when he was building his shadow. In consequence, they had to dig drygulcher lead out of him on four different occasions. The last slug they took out of his back, low down above the hips, and it was that one which caused his legs to go bad as he grew older, and he used you to handle so many of his affairs for him.

"So there you are, boy. If you're smart, you'll watch the trail ahead and you'll watch the trail behind and you'll keep an eye on the country on both sides at all times. Don't be too proud to crawl on your belly, when it could mean your skin if you walked straight up. There's your answer and it's the only one. Remember me kindly . . . !"

Joe Hazle slapped Yeager on the shoulder and turned into Tealander's store while Yeager went on over to the Lucky Seven where he found Mike Breedon alone and half asleep behind the bar. Breedon started to set out bottle and glass, but Yeager shook his head.

"Only a question, Mike. When Miles Grayson and Johnny Richert were in here yesterday, did they do much talking with anybody?"

"Not that I could see. They never opened up at all until you showed later on. Hell! They hardly spoke to me, outside of just enough to order up a bottle, which they took off in a corner by themselves. Why do you ask?"

"Just wondering at something Jack Cardinal said, is all. Thanks, Mike."

A few minutes later, Yeager left town, putting his horse to a long, swinging jog through an afternoon heat which rendered up a dry and biting pungency from a baked, dusty earth and blanketed the desert's far flatness with shimmering haze. His destination was the lower Double A spread, and while still a good three miles short of it he met up with the Lancaster brothers, Abe and Dan, heading townwards. These were a pair of solid, trustworthy riders who faced him in a troubled bewilderment. They had been, it seemed, down at the Indian Springs line camp overnight and returned to find headquarters virtually deserted except for Frenchy Dubois, who was patrolling the premises with a loaded Winchester.

"Where the hell is everybody and what's going on, Hugh?" Abe asked. "All we could get out of Dubois was that Fletch Irby was set to make a lot of changes. Dubois was so damn smug and surly about it, Dan and me are wondering if we still got jobs."

"You got them," Yeager assured him. "There are some changes due, all right, but Fletch Irby isn't going to make all of them. And neither is Frenchy Dubois. You boys go on along to town and unwind for an hour or two. Then head back to the ranch and sit tight until you hear from me. Right now I'm off for a little matter of understanding with Frenchy Dubois."

Leaving the main trail he cut due east to the Shoshone Hills, whose open lower slopes ran smoothly except for an occasional shadowed gulch or dry wash. In the spring this was fat range, but now it was sere and dry and lay ocher yellow in the sun. Yeager held his mount to a walk, so no lift of dust would mark his passage.

With a thorough knowledge of this country he worked a careful way to the rear of the ranch layout. Once, in a deep gulch that hid him and his horse fully, he hauled up, fretful in his saddle. He wasn't used to skulking like this — like some damn calf-stealing coyote — and it went against his grain.

Still and all, as Joe Hazle had advised, a man

69

was smart who guided himself with common sense. This was no time to ride too straight up and proud in the open when somebody like Frenchy Dubois — suspicious and definitely hating — could be looking over the sights of a Winchester from some hidden corner. If a man used his head, his chances of staying alive were good. But if he didn't, then he could be so quickly dead! That was how Joe Hazle had put it. And he should know, as he'd been behind a law badge for a long time. . . .

Finding some comfort in this reasoning, Yeager swung his shoulders and went on.

There was another gulch directly above headquarters. He ground-reined his horse here, took off his spurs and drifted quietly in on foot, using a corral fence for shelter. Of a sudden, as strange a sensation as he had ever known held him. It was instinctive, sensory, a warning to prickle his nerve ends and turn him wary and alert as an animal. Had he been a dog, he thought tautly, his roach would be bristling and he'd be growling deep in his throat. A knifing sense of danger was that strong . . . !

For some time he stayed just as he was, looking and listening. As Abe Lancaster had said, the place appeared deserted. Right now the only living things in sight were half a dozen horses dozing in the shade of a feed shed and a scatter of blackbirds fluttering about the overflow puddle of a watering trough in the same corral. Yet Abe had also said Frenchy Dubois was somewhere around, acting mean and smug. And Frenchy Dubois was the one man Yeager had come to see.

How to locate him . . . ?

Wherever he was, if on the watch Frenchy's main concern should be the town trail, the usual way of outside approach. And after a considerable wait, Yeager knew he had to gamble on this probability. Yonder, beyond some seventy yards of open ranch yard, was the blank rear wall of the bunkhouse. A long, long trip under the present circumstances, and the man trying it would be a sitting duck should Frenchy Dubois happen to see him. Even if he made it safely, decided Yeager bleakly, he was going to age a little along the way. . . .

He drew his gun and made the crossing, low and fast. Safely against the rear of the bunkhouse, he waited and listened again. Time stretched on and the world lay still, until abruptly, up front someone cleared his throat and spat. Just past the bunkhouse corner was a window and in this Yeager had his cautious look. Satisfaction seeped through him. Slouched at ease in a chair, Frenchy Dubois was outlined against the open rectangle of the bunkhouse door. He was far enough inside to be hidden from anyone approaching along the town trail, while having a good view of the outside himself. Across his knee lay a rifle.

Yeager ducked under the window and went slowy ahead to the forward corner of the building, again to pause while figuring his next move.

Almost at once he had his answer, as a stir of warm air curling past the corner brought the smell of cigarette smoke.

Frenchy Dubois, Yeager knew, was a chain smoker, and except when eating and sleeping, was never without the stub of a Durham cigarette pasted on his lip. No sooner did he discard one butt then he'd start rolling a fresh smoke. So, aware of this, Yeager now waited for this break.

It came presently. The butt of a brown paper cigarette flipped aside, spun from the bunkhouse door to join several others like it in the dust. Timing Frenchy's subsequent moves as closely as he could, Yeager made his gamble. He wheeled to the open door, gun leveled ahead of him. Past the gun he saw Frenchy's startled eyes bulge, then narrow in trapped desperation. For both of Frenchy's hands were busy, one about to return a half-empty sack of Durham tobacco to a shirt pocket, the other holding a newly rolled cigarette to his lips as he licked it into shape. He dropped both items and grabbed at his rifle, but stopped the move at the menace in Yeager's harsh warning.

"Go through with it, Frenchy, and you're dead! I didn't do all this Injuning up on you just to play nice. I'll take that rifle myself!"

With his free hand he lifted the weapon and tossed it aside. "Who were you waiting for, Frenchy — me, maybe? I think so. Now come on out here in the open. Easy does it!"

Sullen, black eyes smoldering, Frenchy came out. He didn't have a belt gun, so now Yeager holstered his own weapon.

"What the hell's the idea of all this?" Frenchy blurted. "Why would I be waiting for you?"

"Now who else would you wait for, except maybe Sam Carlock?" Yeager mocked. "Which reminds me, speaking of old Sam . . . !"

He cuffed Frenchy across the face, dropping him to his knees. "A little something for old Sam," Yeager ground out. "I understand that after Fletch Irby — now there's another big, brave soul — knocked Sam down, you used your boots on him. And if there's any lower business than using your boots on a man better than twice your age — and him on the ground — you tell me what it would be. So I've just started on you, Frenchy. Get up and take it!"

Dubois started up, hesitated and dropped back. "I only did what Irby told me to do. . . ."

"Then you shouldn't have listened," Yeager cut in stonily. "On your feet!"

Dubois shook his head. Yeager grabbed him, hauled him up and slapped him down again.

"When I started, I didn't think I'd really enjoy this. But remembering how old Sam looked when he came in at the Sheridan Bench headquarters, I'm beginning to. Get up, you dirty whelp, or so help me, I'll boot you up . . . !"

This time Frenchy did come up, with a desperation and quickness that enabled him to land a couple of wild, flailing blows, one of them bringing the salty taste of blood to Yeager's lips. He tried to drive a knee into Yeager, to kick a leg from under him. But Yeager clubbed him under the ear and put him down for a third time. Rolling and scrabbling, Frenchy went for his rifle.

Yeager got there first, snatched the weapon away and after jacking the lever back and forth to empty it of cartridges, with a single hard swing smashed the gun to uselessness against the bunkhouse wall.

"So much for that," he said harshly. "Now we begin the other again, because you haven't near paid for what you did to Sam Carlock. On your feet!"

Frenchy wouldn't get up. Convulsed with a defiant hate he stayed on his hands and knees. Yeager urged him with a boot toe but it did no good. All Frenchy Dubois would do was shift a little then stay as he was, peering upward with a couched but servile savagery. Again Yeager hauled him up, right fist cocked for another blow. He couldn't deliver it. Strong as the urge was to break every bone in this cringing fellow's body, Yeager found he couldn't continue to punish him when he refused to even protect himself. It was too much like kicking around a snarling and vicious, but cowering, defenseless cur dog. Growling his disgust, Yeager threw Dubois aside.

"I should wring your damn neck," he stormed. "Instead I'm running you out of the country.

You're leaving this range for good, Dubois. You're going far and staying so. Should you try to sneak back, then you'll never leave. Maybe I can't bring myself to maul a yellow rat with my hands, but I can always shoot one on sight. Now you know. Saddle up and start traveling!"

V

Back when Lorie Anselm was still a slim, eleven year old in calico shirt, brown bib overalls and small half-boots, all flashing eyes and tousled, windblown hair as she scurried about the ranch in her various childhood projects, Buck Abbott rode purposefully to town one day and sought out Helen Stent at the hotel.

"Helen," he rumbled, "it comes to me that the youngster Dean Anselm left in my care will soon be moving out of overalls into dresses. When she does, an old hard-shelled buffalo like me won't be much comfort to her. She'll need someone like you, an older person of her own kind to visit with and confide in. I'll take it mighty kindly if you'll give the youngster and me a helping hand when those days arrive. I'll be more than happy to pay whatever it's worth to you."

Helen Stent's reply was quick, emphatic and indignantly explicit. "All that could keep me from it, Buckley Abbott, is for you to mention payment again. You should know she can come to me any time, anywhere. Also, if you'd know the truth of it, I've been wondering when you'd get it through your head to let me have a hand with Lorie."

So that was how it had been, with Helen Stent like a second mother through Lorie's growing up years. Now, on this particular hot afternoon, from a hotel parlor window, she watched Lorie ride into town with Hugh Yeager, saw them talk for a moment on the hotel steps. After which Yeager went off down street while Lorie came slowly in.

There was a certain room Lorie always used when staying in town. She climbed directly to it now without announcing her arrival, which was not her usual way. After giving her a few minutes to herself, Helen Stent knocked at her door. Lorie was hunched on the edge of the bed, staring with shadowed eyes at the faded rosebuds of the wallpaper. Helen Stent took a seat beside her.

"Troubles, honey?"

Lorie nodded gravely.

Helen Stent slid a comforting arm about her. "Tell me."

Lorie did so, soberly at first, but with a flash of anger showing as she detailed the mistreatment of old Sam Carlock and the events that led up to it.

"That Fletch Irby," she ended furiously. "I've hated and mistrusted him ever since we were kids on the ranch, and he'd catch butterflies and pull their wings off, just to make me cry. Yes, even then I despised him. Now. . . !"

77

"You rode in with Hugh Yeager," Helen Stent said. "Does he know about this?"

Lorie nodded vigorously. "I always tell Hugh everything. He's going to keep Sam Carlock on at the upper ranch. And he insists on seeing to it that my half-interest in the lower ranch is properly looked after."

"Well then," soothed the older woman, "things should work out. Too bad Hugh wasn't on hand to defend Sam Carlock."

Lorie hunched lower, her woes increasing. "Fletch Irby wouldn't dare threaten me or hit old Sam with Hugh present. Which is just the trouble. Hugh wasn't there — but someone else was — and did nothing about it . . . !" Her voice broke slightly.

Now Helen Stent understood completely. Her encircling arm tightened. "Ben Hardisty was there?"

"Yes, he was. And did nothing except talk. He also allowed Fletch Irby to cut him off like he was speaking to a dog. Helen, right then something happened to me. Looking at Ben, it was like seeing a stranger. That scared me. Now I don't know what to think, because I can't understand how he could be that way. Old as he is, Sam Carlock didn't hesitate to stand up to Fletch Irby. But Ben — Ben . . ." The words ran out in a little gulp of misery.

"Sure you're not judging too quickly?" reasoned Helen Stent. "Mere physical courage is never full measure of any man's true value.

Some of the most worthless ones have it because it comes easy for them. Other and better men are not always built that way. There is plenty of truth in the saying that the bravest man is the one who fears but goes ahead just the same."

"I know," Lorie said miserably. "Only — Ben didn't go ahead. All he did was — talk!"

"Ben Hardisty is the man you fell in love with — the man you planned to marry. Remember that."

"I know that," Lorie admitted softly. "Which is what hurts. I'm remembering that — and also other things."

"Such as?"

Lorie flushed. "Why is it, always in time of trouble, I find myself turning to Hugh Yeager?"

Helen Stent laughed. "That's easy, child. Hugh's the same sort Buck Abbott was — big, rugged, dependable, full of comforting strength. Their kind always inspire confidence, and attract others needing shelter."

"There was a time," explained Lorie carefully, "when I thought I could feel that way about — Ben. But now . . . !" She shook her head dismally.

Helen Stent stood up. "You need to get your mind off yourself. And I've got some pies to bake for supper. I can use your helping hand. Come along. You'll probably feel much better in all ways tomorrow."

There was, Lorie found, wisdom in the panacea Helen Stent offered. The big, high-ceilinged hotel kitchen, reasonably cool in spite of the cooking range and the warmth of the day out-side, had always been a favorite retreat with all its good fragrances of living and cooking, of cof-fee and spices and all such honest, homey things dear to any feminine heart. Nor was Helen Stent's wise and busily capable presence the least of its comforts. It was, Lorie mused as she mixed and rolled pie dough, a place where one felt both useful and secure.

By the time half a dozen pies were cooling on a shelf by an open window, powder blue dusk cloaked Piegan Junction. Riders came in off the desert and down from the hills in a tearing rush and called back and forth along the street before crowding into the Lucky Seven where Mike Breedon faced another busy night.

Andy Stent lit the hotel lamps and other lights threw splinters of yellow glow against the deep-ening dark. Sparrows cheeped sleepily in the poplar trees and hoof-churned dust drifted. Lorie closed the window by the pie shelf as the supper crowd began drifting in.

While Helen Stent handled things in the din-ing room, Lorie kept matters moving in the kitchen and in the rush of this useful busyness was forgetting some of her personal miseries un-til, with the supper hour about done with, Helen Stent came in with a load of empty dishes and dropped a disturbing remark.

"Ben Hardisty's out there. Wants to see you. If

you feel you've something to settle with him, best get it over with."

Ben Hardisty sat at the same table they'd occupied that morning when Fletch Irby first made his buying out talk. He stood up as Lorie approached, showing a small, protesting smile.

"You needn't look at me that way, Lorie. I'm sorry about that trouble out at the ranch. But I never did believe in trying to brawl my way through any argument where common sense offered a better approach. Men were given brains to reason with. Now let's calm down and talk things out."

He held a chair for her and she settled into it slowly. "What is there to talk about, Ben?"

"You and me, mainly. Our future. What to do about it. I warned you that any attempt at a working partnership with Fletch Irby would end exactly as it did — in a stupid, senseless row. There's only one intelligent way out of this, Lorie. It is — sell to Irby."

She studied him searchingly, then shook her head. "No, Ben. Like I said before, I'll not sell to Fletch Irby."

Frowning, Hardisty leaned forward against the table.

"That's not being smart. Aside from the fact that you have no use for the man, what other reasons could you have?"

"Two of them, Ben. The first is that Fletch Irby hasn't enough money to pay what my share is worth."

"How do you know he hasn't?" demanded Hardisty.

"Where would he get it? Only by selling his share, if he could find someone to buy it. Which would get him — what? Even if he did have it, it would make no difference. I am not selling to him!"

Hardisty swung his shoulders impatiently. "All right — all right! So you're determined to hang on to an impossible situation. Irby's already run most of your old riders off the ranch. If he brings in some of his own to replace them, what do you think will happen to your interests? Who do you think they'll take their orders from? Not from you."

"My interests will be looked after," Lorie told him steadily. "Hugh Yeager is going to take care of that. Also, I've promised Hugh faithfully that I'd never sell to Irby."

A growing anger flushed Hardisty's cheeks and his lips pulled thin.

"Well now — you don't say! Just how does Mister Yeager rate in something that's none of his business? What right has he, mixing in your affairs?"

"The right of an old friend, Ben. He ran things for Uncle Buck — why shouldn't he run them for me?"

"Because I'm the one who should do that. At least I thought I was."

Again Lorie studied him, very grave, a little sad because she knew she was saying good-bye to something she'd once thought bright, shining and full of beauty. Her answer, though simple and direct, was unconsciously devastating.

"You didn't handle them very well this morning, Ben."

He settled back in his chair, staring at her. And to her he again carried the look of a stranger. She got to her feet.

"I'm sorry, Ben. But I've got some thinking to do about you and me. Since Uncle Buck's passing, my whole world has changed somehow. I can't explain it exactly but it is so. And so many things have changed — so many things."

Now he stood facing her, eyes narrowed, lips twisted. His reply fell jerkily.

"You say — so many things have changed. Well, they sure as hell have . . . !"

He turned on his heel and went out.

Lorie went slowly back to the kitchen. Tears were close, close enough to sting her eyes, but she gulped them back. Helen Stent was sympathetically observant.

"Everything straightened out, honey?"

Lorie shook a forlorn head. "Nothing is. I just don't understand myself. Once, between Ben and me, everything seemed so great. But now . . ."

"If it was really worthwhile, then it will stay worthwhile," Helen Stent comforted. "But if it wasn't really great, now is the time to find it out."

Leaving the hotel, Ben Hardisty headed

straight for the Lucky Seven. He found place at the end of the bar and when Mike Breedon put bottle and glass before him, poured and quickly downed two heavy jolts. He let the impact of these burn their way through him, then poured and put away a third strong four fingers of the liquor. After that the floodgates opened. Near an hour later he lurched out into the street, weaving about uncertainly before locating his horse. Then it took several tries to find a stirrup and drag himself into the saddle. After which he headed homeward through a desert night flooded with the pale silver of moon glow.

Well out in the desert, knowing the place was empty at the moment, Frenchy Dubois hauled in at the Indian Springs Double A line camp to water his horse and fill the canteen slung at his saddle horn. He ransacked the camp for food but found only a little stale coffee, barely enough to cook up a small, tasteless pot of it. While drinking this, he considered the future and found it anything but good.

He'd left Double A headquarters driven by cold fear. But as he put miles between himself and Hugh Yeager and began to feel the safety of distance, the fear gave way to a red and wicked hatred, and the innate cunning in him began to take over and shape his thoughts. What lay ahead for him beyond the desert's distant edge he could only guess at as he had less than two dollars in his jeans. But here, if it wasn't for

Yeager — well, things could be good. They could be very good in fact. For Frenchy had guessed some of the things Fletch Irby had in mind, and if he was able to stay along with Fletch, he could ride high again. Only, there was the shadow of Hugh Yeager across the trail.

More and more the red hatred and the cunning took over. Hell! — Yeager was human, wasn't he? And a bullet at the right time in the right place could take care of him the same as any other man. Only right now Frenchy had no rifle nor even a belt gun. Yeager had smashed his rifle against the bunkhouse wall back at headquarters and had taken over Frenchy's belt gun before sending him on his way.

The basic animal and the simplicity of animal reasoning was strong in Frenchy Dubois. To fear when cause for fear was close, to forget it when it wasn't. And never to quit hating while the cunning grew ever stronger. Guns could be located if a man had a little luck and searched carefully enough. Not a ranch house within five hundred miles but what had a rifle or two somewhere about the premises. Which was what he wanted most. A rifle to lay out with in the timber somewhere near the Sheridan Bench headquarters; to wait and watch a chance when Hugh Yeager came riding. One careful shot — and then a lot of good things could lie ahead. Probably double pay from Fletch Irby, who'd like nothing better than to see Yeager laid away. So how about the closest ranch that would have the rifle he needed? Frenchy considered this proposition carefully and by the time the day ran out, he had his problem figured and rode accordingly.

Ben Hardisty's ranch headquarters was not large, but was well laid out and well built. It was mainly a one man spread, except for the busy seasons of the year when Hardisty would pick up a stray rider or two to help out. The rest of the time he managed and worked the place by himself. These things Frenchy Dubois knew. Also he knew a deep contempt for Hardisty. He'd watched him back down abjectly before Fletch Irby when even that old fool of a Sam Carlock had shown more salt. And though he couldn't ever remember seeing Hardisty carrying a gun, there was sure to be a rifle about the place to work on a stray coyote or put a crippled cow critter or horse out of its misery.

The moon, far enough past half-full to look a little lopsided, flooded the world with its pale radiance when Frenchy came cautiously up to the place. There was no light in the ranch house and no gear on the saddle pole by the corral gate. Frenchy exulted in his luck. With nobody home this would be easy.

He moved boldly about the ranch house, locating and lighting a lamp, then gathering what he wanted. The needed rifle was there all right and it was a good one, in top condition, and there was one full box of ammunition, and another with only two cartridges gone. Frenchy loaded the weapon, pocketed the rest of the ammunition, then went into the kitchen. He'd need a supply of food, for that lay out in the timber on Sheridan Bench might run into a week or more before he got his chance at Hugh Yeager. He found an empty flour sack and stuffed it to fatness from Hardisty's grub supply. Finally he gathered a couple of blankets off Hardisty's bunk.

He put out the lamp, toted his loot out to his horse. He made the sack of food and the blankets into a tight pack and tied it down behind his saddle cantle. Then, when he was about to mount, his horse swung its head and whickered an equine greeting. Out there in the night the dust-muffled clump of hoofs announced an arrival. A mounted figure loomed big in the moonlight, and in clumsy, whiskey-thickened tones, Ben Hardisty laid out his blunt demand.

"Who is it — whatcha want? Hear me — who the hell is it . . . ?"

Panic surged through Frenchy Dubois. Here was the fear again; the fear he thought he'd put behind him. If he was recognized now, and the word got back to Hugh Yeager . . . ! He didn't think any further. There was just one way to make sure he wasn't recognized.

He swung up the stolen rifle. Even had there been only starlight, his target was too close to miss. Now, clothed in moon haze, that target seemed to loom gigantically. The rifle ripped out its hard, flat smash of report, and Ben Hardisty went out of his saddle like a twisted reed.

Frenchy Dubois hit his saddle and spurred frantically off into the stunned night, pursued it seemed by the still rocketing echoes of the shot.

VI

The Piegan Junction bank was a one man affair, and Frank Cornelius held to a strict schedule to keep its affairs in shape. His opening and closing hours were precise; ten in the morning, three in the afternoon. In this way, generally by five o'clock, the day's business would be cleaned up, the vault locked, and he free to drop by the Lucky Seven for a brandy, or stop at the store for the mail and any new items of gossip Duff Tealander had managed to gather.

This day, pausing in the bank doorway for a moment's survey of the street before locking up, Cornelius watched Hugh Yeager ride into town and caught the beckoning gesture which held him for Yeager's approach. Yeager was grimed with trail dust, his face and eyes set in grimness and there was a puffed look to his lips.

"Hate to bother, Frank," he said. "But I've a couple of questions."

Cornelius nodded. "Come on in."

In his office the banker said, "Hugh, you've the look of trouble about you."

Yeager touched his lips where one of Frenchy Dubois's wild swinging fists had managed to land. "This part doesn't matter. What does count is — has Fletch Irby been after a loan lately — a loan big enough to buy Lorie Anselm's share of the ranch? Or is that private information that's none of my business?"

Cornelius smiled slightly. "If he had, I'd have turned him down. In fact, if Fletch Irby was to ask me for a fifty dollar loan, I'd have to think it over first. What's behind this, Hugh?"

"Things are getting mean," Yeager said slowly. "Fletch Irby is forcing the betting." He sketched briefly the events which ended in Lorie Anselm bringing Sam Carlock to the upper ranch. "I brought Lorie to town to stay, then went out to the lower ranch hoping I'd find Irby there and have a damn good straight up and down understanding with him. He wasn't there. But Frenchy Dubois was and sort of hid out with a Winchester like he was set to gulch somebody — maybe me. Which I didn't like. I roughed him up some to make it even for Sam Carlock, then ran him out of the country. Now I'm wondering about a couple of other things. Like this:

"The riders who jumped me in Tealander's alley were complete strangers. I didn't know them. Neither did you or Duff Tealander. Nor did Joe Hazle. So I asked myself, how did they know about the money I was carrying? Something else. When I met up with Jack Cardinal in the Lucky Seven, the first sneering crack he made was to say he understood I was out of a job.

"Well, just three people knew I'd be back from Omaha with the beef payoff: you, Lorie Anselm and Fletch Irby. Certainly neither you nor Lorie spread the word — so — ? And while Irby had made his brag to Lorie and Miles Grayson and Johnny Richert about firing me, none of them relayed the word to Jack Cardinal. Then who did . . . ?"

Concern pulling at his cheeks, Frank Cornelius nodded soberly.

"This comes as no surprise to me, Hugh. Right along Fletch Irby had it figured to one day own Double A — all of it. As Buck Abbott's nephew he thought he had the inside track. The change in Buck Abbott's will really jolted him, but he's raunchy enough and wild-headed enough to work at getting hold of the ranch any-how — and any way!"

"Looks so," Yeager agreed. "Well, however Fletch plays it, that's the way he'll get it. The Jack Cardinal angle has me wondering enough to make me take a little ride over Massacre Pass into the Elkhorn Flat country. That's Jack Cardinal country too, you know."

"Also," added Frank Cornelius sententiously, "damn dangerous country for you just now. Don't ever forget that!"

Yeager hunched a shoulder. "At my age and for the same reason, what would Buck Abbott have done, Frank?"

"Gone in there like a sore-eared grizzly and put Cardinal up a tree."

91

"Just so," Yeager said. "Thereby wangling a couple of needed answers. Obliged, Frank."

Late afternoon shadows were smoking up the aisles of timber when Yeager topped out on the Sheridan Bench and went along to headquarters, where things were quiet enough. Miles Grayson and Johnny Richert were busy at the usual round of day's end ranch chores. In the bunkhouse, Sam Carlock looked rested and better.

"Take it easy until everything is right for you, Sam," Yeager told him. "Later you'll be cooking and keeping a general eye on the ranch while Miles and Johnny and I work cattle. But I want you to know that affairs could start shaping up pretty rough."

"That," vowed the old puncher, "is how I want it. I'll never be caught without a gun again."

In the early dark, Yeager made up a small pack, saddled a fresh horse, strapped a scabbarded Winchester to his saddle and headed for the Massacre Pass Road. He took his time climbing this, topping out in the pass just before midnight with the stars burning coldly and the moon silvering the crests. Well down the far side he pulled off the road into the timber, unsaddled and put his horse on picket, rolled into his blanket and slept until a chill, gray dawn seeped across the world. He crawled from his blanket, stretched, yawned widely and faced the new day.

Just at sunup he rode into Elkhorn Flat, a mean little collection of raw-boarded cabins, a stable and corral, and one larger, two-storied building looming above all the rest.

It had been some time since Yeager was last here, and he saw the place as little different than before, other than more weatherworn. He hauled up before the larger building and searched the world round about with care and wariness before swinging down and looping a rein on the hitch rail. The creaking of the warped and worn planks of the building's porch when he started across them brought the figure of Gabe Norton to the doorway.

Here was a huge man, once raw-boned and craggy perhaps, but now gone badly to fat. A none too clean undershirt clung close to shoulders that were lumped and misshapen. An enormous paunch overflowed a belted trouser top. His features were puffed and doughy, his eyes little flecks of dull lead in pouchy sockets. He stood in a pair of worn, badly scuffed congress gaiters.

Yeager spoke mild greeting. "Morning, Gabe. Still serving meals?"

"Likely so," Norton wheezed, stepping aside and waving him in. "Some time since you were through here last, Hugh."

"Some time," Yeager agreed. "How are things with you?"

The lumpy shoulders shrugged. "They come and they go. Now and then they leave a dollar or two with me. So I make out. You want a drink before breakfast?"

Yeager shook his head. "Just breakfast."

There was a small and sadly battered bar in the place. Also an even smaller room where a man could eat. Gabe Norton yelled a summons to someone out back, then led the way to a table. Breakfast was steak and potatoes, coffee and biscuits, served by a slattern breed woman. She turned a pair of black, suspicious eyes on Yeager as she set the meal before him. But the food was savory and he ate heartily. Across the table from him, Gabe Norton toyed with a cup of coffee. Chewing busily, Yeager indicated the meat on his plate.

"Good beef, Gabe. Critter must have been fat."

Norton's heavy lips quirked and a flicker of amusement showed far back in his eyes. "Not Double A beef, if that's what's worrying you, Hugh."

"Now I'm glad to hear that," Yeager told him evenly. "Because if it was I would worry. Wouldn't like to have to come in here and burn you out, Gabe. Which could happen should any Double A beef move over the pass without me or some of my men driving it."

Gabe Norton's ponderous bulk sagged deeper in his chair. "You," he complained, "talk just like Buck Abbott used to. Yet old Buck's gone while I'm still here."

"In time all men live out their years," Yeager

said. "Buck Abbott did. You'll do the same. But it would be foolish to hurry it, don't you think. And Gabe — has Fletch Irby been through here lately?"

He threw the question abruptly, closely watchful for reaction. It showed, though faintly, a single startled flicker in the slitted, leaden eyes before the curtain dropped. Norton shook his head.

"If he has, I ain't seen him. Though of course I can't spend all my time sittin' on my porch watchin' to see who goes by."

"Maybe Mack Snell does the sitting and watching for you?"

Norton pushed a puffy hand across his face as if he was wiping away all expression.

"Anybody who spends a dollar with me can sit on my porch all he wants, just so he don't bother otherwise."

Yeager chuckled dryly. "Same old Gabe Norton. Big as the side of a barn, but slippery as a greased lizard when you try to pin him down. Well, here's my dollar."

He laid the coin on the table, drained his coffee cup, leaned back and rolled a cigarette. He spoke with a slow but definite emphasis.

"Gabe, things have happened over across the summit. Some folks might figure, with Buck Abbott gone, that Double A is now a fat goose ready for the slaughter. Don't you believe it. Also, don't serve any Double A beef across this table. You do, you'll find it damn tough chewing. Aside from that, I think you and I can get along."

Gabe Norton sat quite still, brooding over this. When his head finally lifted, his eyes held a brighter shine.

"Hugh, ain't you talkin' a mite large? Was I to raise a shout, you could have trouble getting back across the pass with a whole skin!"

Yeager showed him a grin that was hard and direct.

"You might raise that first shout, Gabe. But I promise you something; you'd sure as hell choke to death on the second. Want to try it?"

Norton's glance held for a moment, then slid away. "I'm a peaceful man, which is why I've lived this long. But you surprise me, Hugh. I never figured you one to turn eager with a gun."

Yeager pushed back his chair and stood up. "Men can change, Gabe — depending on circumstances. And now that I've spent my dollar with you, I think I'll sit on your porch for awhile."

Outside he settled into a round-backed chair and surveyed the morning world. Here and there signs of life showed. Thin drifts of aromatic pitch pine wood smoke drifted straight up in the still air from several cabin chimneys. In a far rank of timber a Stellar jay called with racuous jauntiness, then floated across the clearing on swift, swooping wings.

A man coughed thickly and stepped from a cabin door, squinting into the sun. His appearance was startling for it seemed his face was cut in half by a line of white. He coughed again before angling toward the stable and corral. Passing, he threw a hangdog look at Yeager, who at this closer range now was able to identify that line of white for what it really was. Across the man's nose a bandage reached from cheekbone to cheekbone.

The fellow went into the stable and presently from a side opening forked several feeds of wild hay to the horses in the corral. Beside the stable door was a watering trough and Yeager, struck with a sudden and electrifying thought, left the porch, untied his horse and led it over to the trough. The water was stale and scummed and the horse, after sniffing it, swished it back and forth in distaste. Yeager waited with an apparent unconcern, but inside he was strung tight, and when the bandaged one emerged from the stable door Yeager's command hit like a club.

"Hold it, you — right there!"

The fellow went still, staring. Yeager moved in quickly, jammed his gun against the man's ribs and pushed him back inside. The move brought a nasal whine of protest.

"What the hell is this. What do you think you're doing?"

Dropping his free hand on the fellow's shoulder, Yeager spun him around so that he could watch the outside beyond the open door while holding his man at gun point. Satisfied that so far his maneuvering had not aroused any outside interest, Yeager questioned curtly.

"Remember me?"

"No," came the answer. "Never saw you before."

"I think you did," Yeager said. "But it was pretty dark in that alley, too dark for you to recognize me clearly. So I'll name myself. I'm Yeager — the man who got off the train with the money satchel — remember?"

The fellow remembered, all right. It showed in the quick fear that flared in his eyes and the way he cringed from the pressure of the gun against his ribs.

"Yeah," went on Yeager. "And in the ruckus that followed I remember feeling somebody's nose going flat under my fist. So when I saw you with that bandage, I just had to find out if you were the man. Good guess, wasn't it?"

Apparently realizing it would do no good to try and lie, the fellow made surly reply.

"I didn't do nothin' worse to you than you did to me. Ain't no need of stickin' a gun in my ribs. I didn't get away with any money."

"No," Yeager agreed, "you didn't. Not because you didn't try, of course. Even so, I wouldn't hold that against you providing you decide to do a little talking. There are some things I want to know. What's your name?"

"Cruze — Ed Cruze."

"There were three of you," Yeager reminded. "Who were the other two?"

"Jeff Lord and Harry Coe. Jeff got away with

me. I don't know what happened to Harry. I heard some shootin'."

"That's right, you did," Yeager said curtly. "And your friend Coe stayed in Piegan Junction — dead! Now the big question. Who told you I'd get off that train with the money? How did you learn about it?"

There was no immediate answer, so the muzzle of Yeager's gun dug a little deeper. "I finished your friend, Coe. I can do the same with you. You better talk while you got the chance."

"It was Harry Coe who knew," Cruze blurted, flinching. "Jeff and me — we just trailed along."

"And how did Harry Coe know?"

"Some man told him."

"What man?"

"Dunno. Just somebody Harry got it from."

Yeager whirled him, slammed him against the stable wall. "Won't do, Cruze! I want more than that from you. If I have to, I'll gun whip you down to a rag. Come on, God damn it! Who was that man?"

Ed Cruze wilted. "A'right," he mumbled. "It was a feller named Irby, Fletch Irby."

"Now that's real interesting," Yeager murmured, some of the hard tension of the moment easing out of him. This whole thing had been a gamble, a shot in the dark born of the sudden hunch that came to him at sight of this man's bandaged nose. He eased up a little on the gun pressure.

"What was the deal, Cruze? I imagine the big

part of the money was to go to Fletch Irby — right?"

Cruze bobbed his head. "Me and Jeff and Harry were due for a hundred dollars each. The rest was for Irby. Now you know, how's for taking that gun out of my ribs?"

"Sure," Yeager said, and did so. "But you're not done yet. You're due to tell your story to some other people in Piegan Junction. Which means you're riding across the pass with me. You'll stay healthy if you do exactly as you're told. Otherwise . . . !" The gun muzzle dug in once more.

Cruze cringed again, protesting. "I told you what you wanted to know. That should earn me a break."

"You'll get the break when you've told your story again in Piegan Junction," Yeager promised. "After that you'll be free to clear out of the country. But right now you saddle a bronc. I'll be watching every move. Don't make the wrong one!"

Cruze was careful about it. He brought a horse from the corral, put a saddle on it and swung up. Then he headed out along the Massacre Pass Road at a leisurely jog, Yeager moving up beside him.

As soon as they reached timber, Hugh Yeager set a quickening pace. Though he had moved this fellow Cruze out of Elkhorn Flat without any trouble, common sense declared he pay some heed to the back trail, which he did, slow-ing a little now and then to look behind him. On either hand the timber ranked thickly, and a hostile gun forted up in it would be mean stuff. But he had come down the road earlier without any trouble and if any showed now he figured it would come up from the rear.

This was outlaw country. Over the years Buck Abbott had fought back against it, and the fact that so far Double A had held its own was true measure of the outfit's strength. Now, however, there was this new angle of Fletch Irby to reckon with. Even though confident Abbott's original will gave him inside track toward full ownership of Double A, Fletch had schemed to further weaken Lorie Anselm's hold by robbing her of her share of the beef shipment money. Also, in case this did not force her out, he'd have just that much more money toward buying her out. But things had not worked out that way, so there was no telling what Irby's next move would be. . . .

The man had always been thrusting, arrogant, heavy-handed in all things. Now he'd shown himself without scruple when it came to gaining a desired end. He'd done business with this fellow Cruze and two more like him in one shady deal. Which meant he could, or would, do the same with others of similar stripe from this side of the mountains. Even, perhaps, with such as Jack Cardinal. The more a man thought about it the murkier the setup became, and the wider the reach of its possibilities. For if Fletch Irby didn't hesitate at bald-faced robbery, what would he stop at?

Nearing the summit of the pass the timber thinned to a bare backbone of gray basaltic rock which sprawled in slabs or reared up in ragged spines. The road worked a winding way through this stretch of badlands to the gut of the pass proper where, even though the sun shone brightly, the high altitude air was cold enough to build little steaming jets from the nostrils of the panting horses. Where shod hoofs rang sharply crossing a few yards of slab rock, Ed Cruze's horse stumbled slightly and brought words from its rider for the first time since leaving Elkhorn Flat.

"Damn this stretch of country! Just the bare bones of the hills stickin' through and full of the ghosts of dead people. Bunch of Modoc Indians wiped out a whole wagon train of emigrants right here one time. Allus gives me a spooky feelin' to ride through it. I'll take the timber country for mine, any day; where things are alive and growin'. But these damn rocks . . . !"

Yeager grinned mockingly. "To me that sounds like a guilty man's conscience speaking, Cruze. Comes of mixing too much with the wrong kind of people. You'll probably feel better after baring your ten cent soul to folks in town."

With the pass behind them the pace picked up and presently, where the road swung across a jutting point, Yeager could look down past the last sweep of the hills to the far yellow and gray and tan run of the desert. Now, carrying up from there faint as a distant echo, came the whistle of another Overland, wheeling past Piegan Junction.

VII

Any man who patrolled a town week in and week out could become a creature of habit. Joe Hazle was no exception. His office was a cubby a few doors above the hotel and his mid-morning tour started there, timed so he was at the railroad station when the day's first freight rumbled in and switched to the long siding by the cattle pens, making way for the fast-running morning Overland, which would pause only long enough to dump a mail sack or two and drop off an occasional passenger in the shape of a drummer or cattle buyer before racing on into the desert's vastness.

Sound purpose accounted for this brief daily contact with the outside world. It gave opportunity to look over any new arrivals and decide whether they were legitimate or the kind Piegan Junction was better off without. In which case there was no better time than now to advise they get back aboard and keep on traveling.

With the trains gone their respective ways, Joe Hazle would trade a few words with Fred Glenn, the station agent, before circling the outer fringes of town to come down from the upper end and stop at the Lucky Seven for the first cigar of the day. It was during this pause that the saloon doors swung and let in an anxious and hurrying Pete Piett.

"Been lookin' for you, Joe," announced the stubby little livery owner.

The marshal grinned. "Well, you've found me. What's agitating you?"

Pete scrubbed a troubled hand across his chin.

"For the last six months Ben Hardisty has dickered me for a blue roan saddle bronc I've had in my corral. Last week he finally made up his mind and bought the horse. He rode it into town yesterday afternoon. I saw him on it as he passed my stable. Right now that bronc is down at my corral with Ben's saddle still on it. Only Ben ain't in that saddle. Which has me wondering."

Joe Hazle sobered. "Why wondering, Pete?"

The stable owner shrugged. "I can understand a loose and riderless horse trailing back to a corral it had known as home for a considerable time. What I can't figure is why it should be loose and with an empty saddle. Maybe somebody should go find out why, don't you think?"

"Somebody should — and will," Joe Hazle said. "You and me. We'll need a couple of horses."

"Got two already saddled," Pete said.

"Something else to think about, Joe," put in a listening Mike Breedon. "Hardisty was in last night, punishing the bottle heavier than I'd ever seen him before. He was weaving some when he left. I don't know why he put away all that liquor, but it could have got the best of him and piled him up somewhere along the trail."

"Now that could be," Joe Hazle agreed, heading for the door. "Come on, Pete!"

They took the blue roan with them and pushed along at a good pace through the day's building heat. Two miles short of the beginning of Double A range they struck the turnoff to Ben Hardisty's layout, keeping careful watch of the trail ahead and the country on both sides, seeing nothing of account until within a short half-mile of Hardisty's headquarters. From here, Pete Piett pointed at the several ominous black dots circling round and round.

"Buzzards, Joe!" he exclaimed. "See 'em?"

Joe Hazle's answer was to lift his mount to a run, hauling the blue roan along at lead. Most of the buzzards had finished their circling approach and were settled on the corral fence a few yards from the human figure sprawled in the hot dust. When Joe and Pete pounded up, the ghoulish scavengers took off with a heavy flapping of wings, naked, red heads cocked truculently.

"There's a dead man," Pete Piett stated, even as he dismounted. "I can tell it . . . !"

Quickly down on one knee beside the prone figure, Joe Hazle nodded bleakly.

"He's dead, all right; shot through and through."

"For God's sake — who'd do that to him. Ben Hardisty never made trouble for anybody."

"He never did," agreed Joe Hazle. "Still, there's always a reason. You keep those damned buzzards off him while I have a look around."

He prowled the yard and he went through the ranch house, and presently had a fair idea. Sober of face he returned.

"We got to get him across a saddle, Pete. It won't be pleasant."

Between them they managed it, and the blue roan's saddle was no longer empty as they headed back to town. It was a grim, silent ride, with the hot desert spreading harsh and bitter brown on all sides. This same heat had held Piegan Junction torpid and inactive, and they came in unobserved to the warm half-gloom of Pete Piett's livery barn runway. Here they laid Ben Hardisty out and covered him with a blanket, after which Joe Hazle went uptown and turned in at the bank.

Frank Cornelius was a shrewd judge of men and their moods, and when he faced Joe Hazle through the wicket he read something of what was in the marshal's mind.

"What and where is the trouble, Joe?"

Joe Hazle explained briefly. "From the looks of things," he ended, "somebody had raided Ben's grub shelf. His rifle was gone, too. Ben was no hand to lean heavy on a gun, but he did own a rifle. I was in Duff Tealander's the day Ben bought it secondhand. He asked me then to look

107

it over and see if it was worth what Duff was asking. I'd know the gun if I ever saw it again. So, from this and that, along with some hoof sign around the yard, my guess is that when Ben got home last night he surprised the raider, who then shot him."

Frank Cornelius shook a deeply regretful head. How, he thought dismally, could you reconcile a thing of this sort with sound reason? Here was a stretch of country that had been reasonably quiet and at peace for some little time. Then Buck Abbott, a strong man, had died and now a savage malignancy was loose across the land, deeply hurting people who did not deserve to be hurt.

"Who," he murmured, half-aloud, "is going to tell Lorie Anselm?"

"Wondered about that myself," Joe Hazle said gruffly. "Best I could figure was tell Helen Stent first and let her break the word to Lorie. Woman to woman in a case of this sort should be easier than man to woman."

Frank Cornelius nodded. "Also, we'll have to get word to the sheriff's office in Empire City. I once told Haley Lockyear that he should have a resident deputy here in Piegan Junction."

"He's got one," Joe Hazle said. "I've been keeping it quiet, but I got a letter from Haley in my desk, authorizing me to take over outside the town limits any time it became necessary. Which it now has."

Still shaking a regretful head, Cornelius accompanied Joe Hazle to the door, from where he watched Hugh Yeager and Ed Cruze ride into town.

"This," he observed, "will certainly shake up Hugh. Who's that with him?"

Yeager answered this by reining to a stop before them and swinging down.

"Just the two I wanted most to see," he announced briskly. "Frank, Joe, meet Ed Cruze. He has interesting information for you. All right, Cruze, tell these gentlemen what you told me at Elkhorn Flat."

Cruze was even more hangdog than before as he gave out the story of the attempted holdup and of what was behind it. Finished, he looked at Yeager. "Remember the break you promised me."

"You'll get it all in good time," Yeager assured. He turned to Cornelius. "Frank, does that answer one of the questions we discussed yesterday?"

"Completely," Cornelius said. "And it doesn't surprise me overly much. Nothing surprises me any more, what with the way things are going. Joe and I have news for you, too. It's not good. Ben Hardisty is dead!"

Yeager flinched as though struck physically. "What's that — what's that! Ben Hardisty — dead?"

Cornelius said, "Tell him, Joe."

As he listened to the telling, savage feeling pulled Yeager's face into a bleak mask. His words fell harshly.

"May God forever damn Frenchy Dubois! I might have known something like this would happen." Then came bitter afterthought. "Does Lorie know?"

"Not yet," Joe Hazle said. "But what's this about Frenchy Dubois? Where does he figure in it?"

"I gave him twenty-four hours to get clear of any part of this range," Yeager explained tautly. "I busted his rifle and took his six-gun away. He didn't have any grub, either. He's the kind who would pull a trick of this sort. I'm making a big guess, of course, but I'm willing to bet on it. Now, how do I face Lorie with the word?"

"Frank and me, we thought we'd let Helen Stent tell her," the marshal said.

Yeager shook off the suggestion. "It's my chore. If it proves out I'm right about Frenchy Dubois, then part of the blame is mine, and I want Lorie to understand that. I'll go see her now."

He turned to leave, then paused. "You better lock Cruze up, Joe. Make sure we hold him until we can face Fletch Irby with him. What do you think?"

"Necessary," was the brief agreement.

"Is that the break you promised," Cruze protested. "Hell of a note, lockin' a man in jail after he tells the truth!"

"The break comes later, when we've nailed Fletch Irby's hide to the wall," Yeager said. "After that you'll go free to haul out of the country.

You're still getting off easy. All right, Joe — lock him up!"

Over in the hotel, Lorie Anselm was wearying through another tiresome afternoon. Always a vigorous girl, fond of active outdoor interests, confinement of any sort irked her. She had helped Helen Stent all she could to pass the time, but now the long hot hours were dragging.

She was in the hotel parlor, trying without much success to get interested in a book when from a curtained window she saw Hugh Yeager and another man haul up before the bank and talk for a little time with Frank Cornelius and Joe Hazle. After this, Yeager came away from the others and headed for the hotel with long, purposeful strides.

Even at this distance, by the very way he carried himself she could read that his mood was grimly determined. She felt she knew this man about as well as she had ever known anyone. Even better, she mused with a sober sense of guilt, than she knew Ben Hardisty, the man she had once thought of marrying. She'd felt she had known Ben thoroughly, too, until those disastrous moments when Fletch Irby, with his heavy-handed and worded contempt, had reduced Ben so shockingly before her eyes.

She'd thought steadily on this since it happened, trying to find true measure of the depths of her own emotional disillusionment, trying even harder to somehow justify Ben's subsequent words and actions, and not gaining much ground in either direction. Of only one thing was she quite certain, nagging awareness of her own guilt. Completely honest and merciless when in judgment of herself, she'd been at odds and ends ever since the destroying incident took place.

Perhaps in Hugh Yeager's company, she thought now, she'd be able to shuck some of her mental miseries and bolster her own strength with some of his as.she had so often done in the past. So it was with real eagerness she stepped from the parlor into the lobby to greet him. But some of the eagerness drained away as, at close range, she sensed the dark trouble in him.

"Hugh," she asked directly, "what is it? What's wrong?"

He did not answer right away. Instead, he took her by the arm and led her back into the parlor. There he squared her around, holding her glance closely as he spoke with grim directness.

"Lorie, this can be a damned cruel world, full of tears for some. You shed them for Buck Abbott. I hope you've saved some for Ben Hardisty."

At first it did not quite register, but when it did it wrung a soft cry from her.

"Ben — what about Ben? Hugh, are you trying to tell me he's hurt . . . that he's even . . . ?"

She couldn't manage the word, but she read it in Yeager's slow, but definite nod.

She swayed a little and caught at him to steady

herself. The next words were heavy and thick in her throat.

"How — why?"

He told it to her as Joe Hazle had told it to him, at the end adding, "Some of it could be my fault."

He had expected tears, but they did not come. She stood very still, staring past him with eyes big and dark with shock — staring at something beyond the walls of this room and that only she might see. Presently, very slowly, she asked:

"Your fault — how?"

He explained about Frenchy Dubois. She swung her head in quick negation.

"You're guessing there, Hugh. You can't be sure it was Dubois. In any case, you're no way to blame."

Looking at her, some of the shadow left his eyes. There was about this girl a warm and appealing honesty. Now also, a poise and strength to amaze him. For though recognizing her great and real regret he still saw no sign of tears. Seeming to read his thoughts here, she straightened her shoulders and moved away.

"If tears would do any good, I'd shed them. But they never bring anyone back, do they? This I have to accept and get used to. No one can help me there, I'll have to reason it out by myself. But for bringing the word so directly — thanks, Hugh!"

Out at the lower Double A headquarters, Abe

and Dan Lancaster were trying to figure the present status of the ranch and its workings. As Hugh Yeager had ordered on the trail the day before, they had gone on into town, bought a caddy of Bull Durham tobacco from Duff Tealander, then loafed away the afternoon in the Lucky Seven before heading home through a smoke blue dusk.

This time they found the place completely deserted. Even Frenchy Dubois was nowhere around, and what with hungry and thirsty livestock in the corrals, there were chores to do. They took care of these, cooked and ate supper, then spent a restless night waiting and wondering. Now another full day had passed with no word reaching them until, just at sunset, men came riding in, near a full dozen of them, with Fletch Irby in the lead. Aside from Irby, these men were strangers.

Abe and Dan Lancaster were mild men wanting trouble with no one but recognizing it now in the overall looks and attitudes of this crowd, along with the harsh, insolent order Fletch Irby threw at them.

"Get busy in the cook shack, you two! We're hungry, me and my men."

Resentment stirred in Abe Lancaster. Mild and peaceful he might be, but underneath there was tough fiber. So he shook his head.

"Not our regular chore, Fletch. Sam Carlock could cook for a crowd, but Dan and me — we don't know how."

"Good time to learn," rapped Irby. "Get busy!"

"Not now, Fletch. Not now — or ever . . . !"

"Then get off the ranch," bristled Irby. "Clear out. You're fired — both of you!"

Abe gave him a moment of grave appraisal before nodding. "So we're fired. Just as well. But isn't there a little matter of back wages due?"

"Not from me," scoffed Irby. "You never did actually work for me. You worked only for Yeager. Go see him about wages."

"Will do," said Abe coolly. "Also prospects of a new job. Come on, Dan — let's get our gear."

By eight o'clock they were in town. The hitch rails in front of Tealander's and the Lucky Seven were lined with saddle stock.

"Town's sure busy," observed Dan, the younger brother. "Wonder why?"

"Could be the world we used to know is coming apart," Abe told him. "Now to locate Hugh Yeager."

They tried the Lucky Seven. Yeager wasn't there, but Jack Cardinal was along with several of his crowd, apparently feeling quite at home and secure. Over the bar Abe made inquiry of a harried and hurried Mike Breedon.

"Hugh Yeager in town, Mike?"

"Was earlier. Wouldn't know now. Try the hotel. He could be there sitting with Lorie Anselm because of Ben Hardisty."

"What about Hardisty?" demanded Abe quickly.

Breedon gave him the word then moved along

115

the bar, busy with bottle and glass for clamoring customers. Back in the street, Abe stood murmuring.

"Did I say the world was coming apart . . . !"

Over by Tealander's store, Marshal Joe Hazle showed. Abe hurried to intercept him.

"Evening, Joe. Hugh Yeager around?"

The marshal shook his head. "He left for the Bench and the upper ranch. What brings you boys back to town?"

"Hoping to find Hugh and see if we're still working for Double A, or if what Fletch Irby had to say is going to stand."

Quickly, Joe Hazle was all interest. "What's Irby got to do with it?"

"He's out at the lower headquarters with near a dozen hard case strange hands," Abe informed. "Tried to make Dan and me cook for him and his crowd. We wouldn't — so he fired us."

"He still out there?"

"I'd think so. Acted like he'd moved in to stay."

Silent thought held the marshal; then: "You boys go on along to the upper ranch. Tell Hugh what you just told me. And tell him to get in touch with me by noon tomorrow."

Dan Lancaster looked over to the Lucky Seven. "Pretty wild crowd in there, Joe. Kinda startling to see such as Jack Cardinal holding forth among honest men."

Joe Hazle grinned wryly. "What I hear about

116

Cardinal and what I can prove are two different things, Dan. Long as he and his crowd behave while in town, I've no authority to bother them. Not how I feel personally, understand. It's how the law reads."

He watched the brothers leave, then went along to his office. Here he lit a lamp and sat up to his desk. From a drawer he got out a heavy manila envelope which held both a letter and a ball-pointed deputy sheriff's star. He read the letter carefully, although he'd already practically memorized every word. He tossed the star up and down in his hand while staring at the blank wall behind the desk. Presently he sighed and slipped the star into a shirt pocket. After which he put out the lamp and returned to the street to resume his regular patrol.

He was still on watch when, near midnight, Jack Cardinal and his men rode out. Next morning he was up and had early breakfast at the hotel before going down to Pete Piett's livery stable for a saddle bronc. Shortly after sunrise he was on his way out to the lower ranch headquarters. When he came in sight of the place he hauled up for a moment of grave-faced survey.

This, he knew, was not going to be easy. Conceivably, it could end up in gunplay. Joe Hazle had been behind a lawman's badge of one sort or another most of the useful years of his life. He had served the law faithfully and efficiently, always letting its written, specific authority speak for him. He had, over the years, arrested many men for many reasons and had also, on occasion, tangled physically with some of the more stubborn ones. To date his only actual use of his gun had been to lay the weight of it across the head of some particularly troublesome lawbreaker. But so far he had never shot a man — never killed a man. And he hoped he wouldn't have to break that record now. . . .

Smoke climbed from the cook shack chimney. A couple of men were in evidence around the corrals. Another one, hatless and tow-headed, stood in front of the bunkhouse and showed Joe Hazle a hard glint of suspicion as he rode up. To the brief question: "Fletch Irby around?" — the man's answer was a surly jerk of his head toward the bunkhouse.

"Tell him Joe Hazle wants to see him."

The tow-headed one slouched to the door, looked inside and growled something. Then he backed away to let Fletch Irby emerge. Irby was tousled from sleep. He offered no greeting, just yawned widely before making blunt demand.

"What d'you want?"

"You," said Joe Hazle quietly. "I'm taking you to town with me, Fletch."

Irby blinked. "You — taking me to town! What are you trying to tell me?"

"That you're under arrest."

Irby swung off the bunkhouse steps and with his thrusting, underslung stride came in close, staring up with a startled heat.

"You drunk or crazy or both? Hell man —

you're not in town now. You're on open range, with no authority to arrest me or anybody else."

"I got plenty of authority." Joe Hazle pulled back the flap of his vest and tapped the star pinned to his shirt. "This says I'm a resident deputy out of Sheriff Haley Lockyear's office in Empire City. So saddle a bronc and come along."

Beyond the heat in Irby's eyes a sly, narrowed wariness took form. "This," he growled, "sure is interesting. Mind telling me what in hell I'm arrested for?"

"For instigating an attempted robbery. That affair in Duff Tealander's alley the night Hugh Yeager got back from Omaha."

"Now I know you're loco," retorted Irby. "I wasn't even in town when it happened."

"No," agreed Joe Hazle, "you weren't. But the men you hired to do the job were. Three of them by name: Harry Coe, Ed Cruze and Jeff Lord. Harry Coe is dead, he came off second best when he tried to gun Yeager. I don't know where Jeff Lord is. But I sure know where Ed Cruze is, and he's told me and some others all about the whole shifty deal. He'll also have the chance to tell it again to the proper court authorities."

"Cruze, you say?" Irby blurted. "Don't know him. Just where is this Cruze hombre?"

"Where you're going — jail!"

Again Fletch Irby yawned and stretched, arms lifted and spread. The grin he showed was more defiant leer than anything else.

"If it wasn't so early in the morning I'd laugh like hell. As it is . . . !"

He was moving with the words, making his grab, catching Joe Hazle by the arm and with one dragging swing, hauling him from the saddle and spinning him to the ground. It was unexpected and cat fast, and before Hazle could do anything about it he was down in the dust with Irby lunging and landing on him with bunched knees.

Joe Hazle was no weakling. He was lean and wiry and fit. But this was a wild, burly, powerful brute of a man who landed on top of him and those bunched knees, driving into him, drove the breath from him in a strangled gasp and left a crushing pain behind. Then there was one clubbing fist mauling at him and another grabbing at his gun. Joe Hazle made a try for that gun himself, but that clubbing fist crashed into his face, near stunning him. The gun was torn from his fingers and Irby tossed it aside with a triumphant yell.

"Take care of that, Whitey!"

The tow-headed puncher caught up the weapon and watched as Irby, the brute in him turned wild now, slammed his fist again and again to Joe Hazle's face and jaw. There was a rampant, mad animal savagery here that made the puncher, Whitey Mendell, step up and drop a restraining hand on Irby's shoulder.

"You aim to kill him, Fletch, there's easier and quicker ways. Remember, he's packin' a star. Best think about that!"

Irby, clenched fist lifted for another crushing blow, held it so for a moment then dropped it back to his side. He pushed to his feet and looked down at the man he had punished so mercilessly. Beaten to insensibility, Joe Hazle lay limp and still, head twisted to one side, features smeared with crimson. Irby came around on Whitey Mendell and gave a hoarse order.

"Get a bucket of water!"

When this came he splashed it across Joe Hazle's face and chest, and it drained off to puddle in the dust. Joe Hazle stirred, groaned softly, rolled over and came up on one elbow staring dazedly about, one eye already swollen shut, the other just a narrowed slit between puffed lids. Blood dribbled from his nose and the corner of his mouth. He wagged his head slowly from side to side, gathering his wits. It took distinct effort to get to his knees and more of it to lurch to his feet, where he weaved unsteadily. Then his head lifted, his shoulders straightened and in his one seeing eye gleamed a spark of cold, indomitable spirit. He spat a thick clot of blood from his battered lips and mumbled his defiance.

"You got the jump on me that time, Irby. But you're still under arrest. I'm taking you back to town with me!"

Fletch Irby stared in open disbelief. Here was a man he'd just given the wickedest of beatings looking him again in the eye and asserting the authority of the star he carried. This Fletch Irby could not understand. Always his own world had been strictly a physical one, and his reaction to it always purely physical. If anything got in your way, tear it apart, smash it down. Never step around any obstacle or any person you could knock down and walk over. Incapable of any other approach to a problem himself, he could not understand it in others.

"You're not taking me anywhere," he told Hazle harshly. "And you're not fooling me one damn little bit. You're up to your ears trying to help your friend Yeager euchre me out of something I have every right to claim as mine. I'm Buck Abbott's lone blood relative, the only person really entitled to the holdings Abbott left behind him. That fact was written into his first will. Then Yeager and Cornelius and probably that Anselm hussy talked the old fool into writing a new will at the last minute. Now you've stepped into the game to help Yeager. So — to hell with you and your star! Take it back to Haley Lockyear and tell him to mind his own damn business. Nobody — and I mean nobody — is going to cheat me out of what's rightfully mine!"

Joe Hazle heard it all but gave no answer. Raw pain was racking him, his world was spinning wildly and a draining weakness dragged at his knees.

"Take him inside and see that he stays there," Irby told some of the men who had gathered. "Whitey, you and me are taking a ride to town for a little visit with Mister Blabmouth Ed

Cruze. Maybe we can persuade him not to talk so much . . . !"

They gave Joe Hazle more water to rinse his bloody mouth and lave his battered face. After which he flattened on a bunk and lay there quietly, but with moiling thoughts. Deep inside was a raw edge of pain, and deep inside him also a seething anger. Anger at himself for being caught so completely off guard, anger at Irby for the man's arrogant defiance and the brute strength that had crushed him down.

For it belittled a man to be handled the way he had been; it cut him down in his own eyes as well as in the eyes of others. He had played the hand very badly, played it like the greenest of tyros. There was, he thought bitterly, a point at which the written law he had cherished so carefully for so long ceased to work. Past that point a man had to turn pure savage to make his authority stand up.

He wondered darkly if he'd ever have a second chance . . .

VIII

Leaving Piegan Junction shortly before midnight, Jack Cardinal and his several followers moved at a slow, hoof-shuffling jog across the flats to the Shoshone Hills and the first lift of the Massacre Pass Road. At this hour, a moon nearing full spread pale silver glow over desert and hills held in a great soft silence. The spell of it could reach all men, even Jack Cardinal, rough, crude renegade that he was. Feeling the magic of this silent, moon-whitened land he reined in short of the first timber on the hill slope, swung his gaunt, bony shape around in the saddle and looked back across the shimmering run of the desert.

"Pretty," he told his wondering companions. "Almost too damn pretty to leave. Back when I was a kid and smarter than I am now, I'd go out into the meadow on a night like this, lay on my back on a shock of hay and soak up the moonlight while trying to figure what life was all about. That was before I got old enough to rate as important all the things men try to gain, thereby making damn fools of themselves. Well, there's a joker in the deck somewhere for all of us."

Having dispensed this bit of unsuspected philosophy, he rode on into the timber. The Massacre Pass Road crossed the Sheridan Bench range well down toward its southern end, and here a mounted figure waited in a moonlit stretch of open. Cardinal sent a low call ahead.

"Yolo?"

"That's it," came the answer. "We been waiting for over an hour, Jack."

"You must have worked fast," Cardinal said. "How many head you got?"

"Right on fifty. It was easy. Cattle bunch up in these timber meadows for the night."

"Any alarm over north?"

"Bruno Orr rode a circle that way. Everything was quiet. This will put a dent in Yeager."

Jack Cardinal laughed in his near soundless way. "Just the first of several for friend Yeager. Where you holding the cattle?"

"Not trying to. Once we got them started, we figured it best to keep them traveling, slow and easy. It's when you try to push critters fast that they begin hollering and raising hell. We'll soon catch up."

They crossed this meadow and a stretch of timber that was shot through with splinters of silver moonlight and where the air hung heavy with the bovine odors of cattle on the move. Presently they were through the timber into another steadily climbing meadow where the moonlight glinted on the backs and horns of a gather of beef cattle slogging steadily up the road. Riders moved with them, at point, on each flank and in the drag.

Jack Cardinal had his look at the high-climbing moon, sniffed the chilling air thereby judging the elevation, and made his satisfied estimate.

"At this pace, we'll be across the summit by sunup."

They did better than that. Dawn was just a line of gray along the eastern rim of the world when they put the cattle through the rock ribs of the pass proper and started down the other side, the downslope drawing the stock ahead at a faster pace. A short mile from Elkhorn Flat the little herd was shunted to a trail that angled away through the timber.

"Deliver them to Mack Snell on South Fork," Cardinal ordered. "He'll know what to do with them. Later on I'll see you at our own camp. Right now Gabe Norton will want to know about this."

He waited until the last sound of departing riders and cattle was soaked up by the deep silence in the timber, then he went on briskly down the road drawn by the thought of food and drink at Gabe Norton's deadfall in Elkhorn Flat.

The place was scarcely awake when he rode in. Gabe Norton's door was open, and knowing his way around in this place, Cardinal located a bottle behind the bar and poured himself a couple of strong jolts of liquor. He was finishing the second of these when Gabe Norton, ponderous and untidy, plodded heavily in, showing frowning complaint when he saw the bottle.

"Making yourself right at home, looks like."

Cardinal grinned smugly. "Fifty head of Sheridan Bench's best should be worth a couple of drinks, wouldn't you think!"

Norton scrubbed a puffy hand across sleep-gummed eyes. "Fifty head, eh? That's hitting pretty strong."

Cardinal shrugged. "What the hell! Why stop at a nibble when there's a full bite to be had for the taking? I thought the idea was to break Yeager's back as quick as possible. I know that's how Fletch Irby wants it."

Gabe got a glass and poured himself a hefty slug. He put this away at a gulp, pulling his lips tight across his teeth against the raw shock of the whiskey.

"That may be Irby's idea, but it ain't necessarily mine," he wheezed. "In some ways Fletch Irby is all damn fool. He wants to travel too heavy and too fast. He don't take time to see clear through to where a deal can lead, and for that reason how it could end. Which is the sort of thing to get himself — and us — into deep trouble."

"When you're out to break somebody — which we are — you don't just wave at him," Cardinal argued. "You hit him hard, the harder the better."

"Maybe," Norton grumbled. "But sometimes it pays to weaken him down a little before putting out the finisher. That way you got a better show of keeping your own hide all in one piece. Fifty head of cattle moved in a bunch leaves a damn broad trail that's easy to follow. Hugh Yeager ain't blind, and he's no fool. I see him as a damn smart man and, with the chips down, a damn tough one!"

Jack Cardinal shrugged again. "Suppose he follows the trail clear to South Fork. All he'll find are cow tracks, and you can't prove anything by them. You got to find the cows that made the tracks, which he won't do. You been here in Elkhorn Flat for a considerable time, Gabe, but you ain't been out in the country round about like I and Mack Snell have. It's big country, with ten thousand little brush and timber gulches scattered all over hell and gone. So Mack and the boys drop off a few head here and a few head there and unless you knew exactly where to look you'd need an army to find them all. So by and by, he gets tired of looking. And then they're ours."

Norton grunted. "Some more of Fletch Irby's push and trample thinking. You make it sound good, all right. But maybe you better stop long enough to realize this. All Hugh Yeager needs to find is just one head of that fifty to put a rope around your neck and hang you to the nearest tree. My idea was to go at this business easy and careful, so's not to get Yeager mad enough and tough enough and backed by enough weight to ride in here and hang some hides up to dry.

Sometimes I wish we'd told Fletch Irby to stay on his side of the hills and keep his damned schemes to himself. We were doing pretty good without him."

"Not all of us," Cardinal retorted. "Maybe you were, but a lot of us been living on damn lean meat for too damn long. Then Buck Abbott dies, and there's some fat to be had by playing along with Fletch Irby. So me and Mack Snell want a share of it."

"Maybe you'll get it and then again maybe you won't," Norton warned. "Don't ever forget that Fletch Irby's first and main concern is nobody else but Fletch Irby. Should he happen to push Yeager and the Anselm girl out of the picture, like he said he aims to do, and grab all of Double A for himself, the very first thing he might do is up you and Mack Snell and all your kind to the handiest tree to make sure you don't start working on him. Don't you ever figure Fletch Irby is tossing some of that fat your way because he loves you. For he don't!"

Jack Cardinal studied him for a moment, then laughed. "You know, Gabe — you're a suspicious old bastard!"

Norton showed a small, grudging grin. "Let's say I'm too old to fight any other way than with my wits."

Piegan Junction faced the beginnings of another hot day with drowsy indifference. In the little jail behind the marshal's office, Ed Cruze sweated and sulked, impartially cursing Hugh Yeager, Joe Hazle, luck and everything else that in any way contributed to his present state of servitude. There was little comfort to be found where he was, as the jail bunk was narrow and hard and the blankets thin.

Last night Joe Hazle had brought him his supper. This morning it was Andy Stent from the hotel who saw that he had bacon and eggs and coffee, though telling him nothing and looking him over with open distaste. After that the morning hours were empty and slow dragging. Now at last, however, there was a step in the hall leading from the marshal's office back to the jail.

Whitey Mendell had entered town by a careful, circuitous route, thereby arriving at the door of the marshal's office unnoticed. He made a quick and careful survey of the street, then slipped inside. From a desk drawer he rummaged some keys and went back to the jail and had the briefest of words for the startled, eager prisoner.

"You don't know me, Cruze. But I'm here to get you out of this place. Keep quiet and do as you're told!"

Cruze did not argue. All he wanted was out, and he ducked along at Whitey's heels down to the cattle pens where two horses waited. Once back in a saddle he felt so free he wanted to yell his exultation. Instead, he pushed up beside Whitey Mendell as they cut across the railroad tracks and headed on out into the desert.

"Where we goin'?" he wanted to know.

"Big Sandy drywash," Whitey said. "Somebody there wants to see you."

"Who wants to see me?" A shade of uneasiness touched Cruze.

"Does it matter?" returned Whitey. "You're out of jail, aren't you?"

"Yeah," Cruze admitted. "But I'd kinda like to know before I go any further." He reined his mount to a slower pace, his uneasiness increasing. "I like the idea of cutting for the hills better."

Whitey's hand whipped across his body and Ed Cruze found himself looking at the muzzle of a gun.

"I guess," murmured Whitey Mendell, "we go on out to Big Sandy!"

Big Sandy drywash was an eroded, steep-sided arroyo which writhed a crooked, roughly east-west course some two miles beyond the railroad. In winter it would hold water, but in summer it was a parched depression, floored with alkali-whitened sand and touched with a scatter of gnarled, weatherbeaten cottonwood trees. At best it was hostile country, and what with the threat of Whitey Mendell's gun and all, now that they reached the rim of the arroyo and he saw who it was waiting in the thin, mottled shade of one of the cottonwoods, Ed Cruze became a hunched, fear-stricken figure. For there was no mistaking that square, blocky shape looming so dark and threatening in the saddle.

Fletch Irby!

Cruze's thoughts spun frantically. If Fletch Irby had known he was in jail, then he must also have known why he was being held there! The fear in Cruze mounted until it became a pressure gripping him by the throat and stirring him to a frenzy of desperation.

East and west twisted the wash, high-banked, floored with sand. Behind him was town, and no place to hide. But straight ahead there was a break in the far wall of the wash and once through that lay open desert, and if a man found any luck at all and his horse was fast enough and had enough bottom, then a man might race to safety.

This was as far as Ed Cruze's thoughts carried him before he lifted his mount to a run, straight across the wash for that break yonder. He crouched low, laying out almost flat along the neck of his straining mount, wondering frantically if he was going to get a bullet in the back and how it would feel. But there was no shot, only a hard, bursting yell from Fletch Irby and then the pound of pursuing hoofs.

Cruze reached the break in the arroyo wall, but within a hundred yards beyond, knew he had no chance. This horse they had brought for him had neither the necessary speed or bottom. A desperate glance over his shoulder showed Irby bearing down on him, gaining remorselessly. He wondered again why no shots had come his way. Maybe Fletch Irby wanted nothing except a talk, after all. . . . It was a good thought and it hauled

Cruze up straighter in his saddle. Maybe if he didn't try to run. . . .

He half turned with the thought. Which was when a noosed rope, thrown with a quick, sure flip, came hard around his neck and tightened there. Irby threw a dally on his saddle horn and swung his racing horse away at an angle. The rope tightened with a snap, yanking Cruze brutally from the saddle, turning him end over end and landing him in a wild tangle of flailing arms and legs. With another hard yell, Irby spurred his horse through a wide, circling run that ended back in the wash. What lay now at the end of his rope was a clutter of torn, shredded clothes inside of which was the broken, shattered wreck of what had once been a man. . . .

Whitey Mendell had a brief look before turning away, his jaw pulled taut and hard. "One clean shot would have saved all that!"

"What's wrong with this?" Irby demanded. "I call it the best medicine in the world for people who talk too much."

Whitey did not reply but had inner words for himself. "This man, for God's sake, ain't human! He's crazy. He enjoyed doing that. I got to get away from him. First good chance that comes — I got to get away . . . !"

Irby glimpsed the look on Whitey's face and exclaimed roughly, "What the hell! Ain't you ever seen a dead man before?"

"Not that kind," Whitey admitted.

With a gesture of impatience, Irby twisted in

133

his saddle, glance searching the banks of the drywash. Some hundred yards along a spot looked about right and he rode to it, the shattered, dragging body of Ed Cruze furrowing the sand. With his horse held tight against the bank, Irby maneuvered until the grisly bundle at the end of his rope rested close under the bank's overhang.

He flipped the rope, loosening the noose until it slipped free. He coiled the rope, hung it to his saddle horn, then dismounted and climbed to the top of the cutbank. Here he stamped and kicked until sun-baked chunks of the bank began to break and fall. Once he got it started, the earth sloughed off more and more freely until it became a dusty cascade. And presently, no visible sign of Ed Cruze remained.

Irby left the bank in plunging strides, and when once again in his saddle, showed Whitey Mendell a wicked grin.

"Neat, don't you think, Whitey? Also, prime medicine for whoever tries to sell me out. Which everybody better remember! Now let's get back to the ranch."

In the chill gray hour of very early dawn and under widely different conditions, two men built breakfast fires in the Shoshone Hills. Sam Carlock started his fire in the cook shack of the Sheridan Bench Double A ranch. The other one was a thin, tapered glow on the cramped floor of a timber-shadowed gulch. Hunched on his heels, hands spread to the meager heat of this blaze, was Frenchy Dubois.

After the Ben Hardisty shooting, Frenchy rode the desert blindly until he had shaken off the worst of his fears, after which he turned back into these hills to this remote hideout. It was strictly a siwash camp, barren and scanty of comfort, and Frenchy's mood was sour and vengeful. Tucked into one edge of the fire a battered coffee pot steamed and across from it bacon sputtered in an equally battered frying pan. Waiting now for the coffee to turn over and the bacon to crisp, Frenchy reviewed the state of his affairs and found them as barren as this camp.

Misfortune had started when Hugh Yeager surprised and disarmed him at the lower ranch. Then, to add insult to injury, Yeager had slapped him around with contemptuous ease before smashing his rifle and ordering him out of the country. Which was bad enough. But then came the even fouler break of luck, the affair with Ben Hardisty. Over the outcome of this, Frenchy had no feeling or regret at all, save an unsatisfactory, empty sympathy for himself.

Through cold, sleepless hours in this hardship camp, he tried to figure his next move. One thing was entirely certain. If he hoped to regain any favor at all in Fletch Irby's eyes after fumbling his chances so badly at the lower ranch, then he had to make a second try at Yeager and make it good . . . !

Frenchy wolfed his bacon and gulped his scalding coffee. The hot food tied him together, firmed up his thoughts. On occasion, while Buck Abbott lived, Frenchy had spent some time at the Sheridan Bench headquarters, working cattle, and in consequence was acquainted with the layout of the ranch and the land close about it. Now, in the smoke of one of his interminable Durham cigarettes, he visualized the place and fixed in his mind just how he would go about another try at Hugh Yeager. He looked at the rifle propped against his saddle, the rifle that had belonged to Ben Hardisty and the gun that had killed him. One good shot from it at the right time and in the right place would take care of Hugh Yeager and solve all his own problems and those of Fletch Irby.

Yes, that it would do! So — why not . . . ?

Knowing a thin edge of excited anticipation, Frenchy pushed to his feet and began stamping out his fire.

In the cook shack of the Sheridan Bench ranch, moving slowly but with steady purpose, old Sam Carlock stoked the big stove anew and heated water to wash the breakfast dishes. Breakfast proper was a full hour gone and the sky in the east was showing the warm rose flare of nearing sunrise. Now that he was able to earn his keep again, Sam was feeling much better. Hugh Yeager had told him to take his full ease for another day or two, but Sam was a tough, grizzled old man with a tough sense of pride, and if the job of running the cook shack was his, then run it he would. And to hell with the aches and pains!

Last evening the Lancaster brothers had ridden in with word of their experience with Fletch Irby at the lower ranch, and at breakfast Yeager had ordered his crew out in pairs to ride the far limits of the Bench range and work up a rough estimate of the number of cattle it held. For himself, Yeager had headed for town, as Abe Lancaster had reported that Marshal Joe Hazle wanted to see him there. So now Sam had the headquarters to himself, and the responsibility of keeping a careful eye on things pleased him mightily.

Wise in the ways of this range world and of the men who rode across it, Sam Carlock's thinking was realistic. As he saw it, what with the word Hugh Yeager had brought of Ben Hardisty's violent death and the way other matters were shaping up, powder smoke would surely roll again before the range turned healthy once more. Therefore it behooved a smart man to check on available armament on the ranch. The Winchesters that had been on the rack in the main room of the house were now riding in the saddle boots of Miles Grayson and Johnny Richert. But the old Sharps buffalo gun that had been Buck Abbott's favorite was still at hand, together with a fair supply of long, lethal-looking cartridges.

Sam hefted the big rifle, sighted it through a

shot out window, then grinned bleakly. Let the trouble come. Long as he had this rifle he was ready for anything.

Outside sounded the skirl of approaching wagon wheels and the tramp of hoofs. Sam moved to the open door and watched Soddy Neff pull up in a spring wagon loaded with a new front ranch house door and several glassed window sashes. Straightening up on the wagon seat, Soddy eyed Sam and the rifle uncertainly.

"If'n you're expectin' any shootin' trouble to show, then I'm headin' the hell right back out of here, pronto! I'm here to do some fixin', not fightin'."

Sam chuckled. "Nothing to worry about, Soddy. Climb down and get at your fixin'. How's for a cup of coffee first to speed the job."

Mollified, Soddy climbed down. "That sounds better. Me, I'm all for peace and quiet."

Later, with Soddy busily sawing and hammering, Sam resumed his kitchen chores, pausing every now and then for a look out the window at the big, dead-topped ponderosa pine tree that stood on a humped up little knoll some two hundred yards back on the hill slope above the ranch house. In a crotch of the tree's dead top, a hawk's nest formed a high dark clot against the sky, and the coming and going of the parent birds with food for their young, had become a thing of deep interest to Sam. Their sure grace as they came swooping in on fast, curved wings, rodent prey gripped in their talons — their shrill crying — all touched a responsive chord in old Sam, who had lived long in the world of wild things and liked it so.

Yesterday the birds had come and gone with complete confidence, settling in swiftly and without hesitation. Earlier this morning they did the same. But now, of a sudden, things were different. They no longer made that fast, sure approach and quick, clean landing. Now they circled warily, and if they alighted at all, it was with a hesitant fluttering before being quickly aloft again. Also, it seemed to Sam that their wild crying carried a note of protest against some kind of intrusion.

As he worked, Sam thought on this and the more he thought the more concerned he became. Something sure was bothering those wary, sharp-eyed birds. What might it be? He surveyed the immediate area carefully several times but saw nothing out of the way. Still and all, the hawks must have as their shrill protest went on and on.

Out front, Soddy Neff was busy working at fitting the new door to the ranch house. And, mused Sam, with a sharpening concern — why was Soddy there doing such a job? He was there because hostile night riders had shot up the old door. Now could some of their kind be skulking out there by the big pine for some further nonfriendly purpose . . . ?

Well now, by God, Sam decided, maybe it wouldn't be a bad idea at all to find out! With this decision came also the plan on how to go about it.

He got the ax off the chopping block by the back door and carried it around to the front where stood Soddy Neff's wagon.

"How's for borrowing your team and wagon for half an hour, Soddy. There's a pitch pine stump back along the road a piece and I want to get some slabs off it. That kind of kindling sure helps starting the fire on a cold morning."

"Sure," said Soddy, shouldering a new window sash and carrying it around a corner. "The rig belongs to Pete Piett and he'll never know the difference."

Sam laid the ax in the wagon, brought out the Sharps buffalo gun and a handful of cartridges, stowed these in the rig too. Then, donning a hat, he climbed in, reined the team around and set off down the road, apparently on some peaceful errand. He drove a good half mile and went through sheltering timber before pulling off the road and tying to a jack pine sapling. He slipped a cartridge into the breech of the big Sharps, then began a careful circle away from the upper side of the road and around toward the ranch.

He traveled fast until reaching a spot from which he could glimpse the bare, towering top of the hawk's nest pine. Now he hauled back the hammer of the Sharps, thrust the muzzle ahead at ready and began a careful stalk, prowling along like a gaunt old wolf, intent on prey. Underfoot the forest mold was thick and soft, and by avoiding dead branches his approach was noiseless, so much so he was right on top of a tethered saddle horse before the animal became aware of him. When it did, it let out a gusty snort of alarm.

Sam went quickly down on one knee, partially hidden by a clump of stunted jack pines. Every sense was straining and wire sharp as he brought the rifle half to his shoulder. Just the faintest stir of air came against his face and on it he smelled Durham cigarette smoke before he made out the figure of a man with a rifle coming quickly down the slope of the knoll.

Recognition turned Sam half-breathless. He brought the Sharps all the way to his shoulder and across the sights of it his eyes gleamed bitterly as he remembered so many things. He let Frenchy Dubois get within forty short yards before laying out his flat, harsh challenge.

"You can stop right there, Frenchy — and drop that rifle!"

Frenchy hauled up dead still for a split second. Shock twisted his swarthy features and his black eyes went desperate and wild.

"Drop it!" ordered Sam remorselessly. "I'm not telling you again!"

By the thinning pull of Frenchy's lips he saw what the man was going to do. It wasn't dropping the rifle. Instead, Frenchy swung the weapon with frantic speed, trying for a snap shot. It was the move of a thoroughly desperate, badly stampeded individual staking everything on one long, last gamble.

It was a losing bet.

The bellow of the big Sharps gun rolled through the timber like trapped thunder. The massive slug knocked Frenchy Dubois back a good ten feet.

He never moved after he fell. . . .

IX

Riding into Piegan Junction, Hugh Yeager saw Andy Stent come from the hotel and turn upstreet toward Joe Hazle's office and the jail. Andy, carrying a tray of food, paused as Yeager drew up at the hitch rail, his glance questioning.

"Should you wonder about this," Andy said, "it's grub for that feller in jail — the one with the patch on his nose."

"Always thought Joe Hazle fed his own prisoners," Yeager remarked.

"Joe ate real early this morning, then left town for somewhere," Andy explained. "He asked me to see the prisoner got breakfast."

"Joe say where he was going?"

Andy shook his head. "Sure had something on his mind, though. I figgered he might be heading for Ben Hardisty's place to sort of check up. That's an empty spread now out there, and somebody will have to look after it."

Yeager jumped down and tied his horse. "Lorie Anselm still with you and Helen?"

"Just sittin' down to her coffee when I left," Andy said.

He moved on to the marshal's office. Yeager

looked the town over, saw it empty and quiet, then climbed the hotel steps following the enticing fragrances of hot coffee and food to find Lorie Anselm at a table just off the kitchen door. She looked lonely and troubled and subdued, and he knew a surge of sympathy as he pulled up a chair. What with Buck Abbott's death and the further smash-up of her world over Ben Hardisty's violent end, she'd taken one hell of a licking. Rough on a lone girl, he thought — damn rough. . . .

She showed him a sober yet welcoming glance. "Hugh, I've got to get out of here. Helen and Andy are the kindest people in the world, but I feel so in the way — so useless. I want to go back to the ranch."

"Not a chance," Yeager said. "Not right now, anyhow. Sure this is tough on you, as you never were one to sit around with folded hands. Always had to be up and doing, splitting the wind on a fast horse, giving the crew a hand with the cattle, just pitching in where you felt you were needed. But you can help most now by staying here where I know you're safe and I don't have to worry about you."

A touch of sweetness softened her lips and warmed her glance. "Then you have worried about me?"

Yeager held a hand at a measuring level. "Ever since you were about so high. Always been a puzzle to me how you could change so sudden from a helter-skelter kid into a grown lady."

"And you approve the change?"

His glance was quick, direct and charged with deep, unspoken meaning. He said it all in a single word. "Plenty!"

The kitchen door swung and Helen Stent came in, bearing a steaming cup. "Steak and eggs also, I suppose?"

Yeager shook his head. "Ate at the ranch before I left. Just coffee will be fine."

Helen dropped a fond hand on Lorie's shoulder. "This young lady has been fretting entirely too much. Mentally, she's lashing herself with a whip of thorns and nettles. She must realize that the earth will keep on turning round and round; that the sun will rise and set, and that time is the great healer."

"I know all that," Lorie protested. "But I should be grieving over Ben. In a way, I think I am. Yet, so far, not a single tear to prove it."

"Which," said Helen Stent quickly, "proves you were lost in a dream of romance that wasn't real — more fancy than fact. Had it been the real thing, there'd be plenty of tears."

Helen went away and Yeager switched the subject, telling what had happened to Abe and Dan Lancaster at the lower ranch.

"Fletch Irby's got the bit in his teeth. He's fired all the old crew off the lower ranch and brought in some wild ones in their place. Which, of course, means fight. So the proper place for you, Lorie, is right here."

"A fight," she said slowly. "With you and our

other good men facing the brunt of it. Which I've no right to expect. Maybe I should have listened to Ben, after all. Maybe I should have sold to Fletch Irby. Then you wouldn't have this sort of thing to face."

Yeager lifted his coffee cup. "Things would be no different if you'd given Irby your share. He'd still be after the Sheridan Bench range. Friend Fletch has always been an all or nothing hombre. Right now he's like a bull running wild down a one-way lane, figuring he can smash through any obstacle he meets up with. You can't treat or deal with a man like that — you have to meet them at their own game. Which is a job for men."

She studied him for a moment before smiling gravely. "One way or another you manage to straighten out my thinking. Because you are too kind to say it, I will. It's high time I quit feeling sorry for myself and faced up to the music. Isn't that it?"

Yeager drained his cup and stood up, grinning. "Smart girl! Coming into town, I found I was riding a bronc with a loose shoe, and I got to see Pete Piett about that. Keep that chin up!"

Leaving the hotel, Yeager met Andy Stent returning from the jail, and Andy made grumbling comment.

"That jigger is sure one surly skunk. Didn't even say thanks for the breakfast. What's he locked up for, Hugh?"

"So he'll be safe and handy until he tells certain things to the right people."

Andy grunted and went along. Yeager untied his horse and led it down to the stable where Pete Piett was busy cleaning stalls. Pete listened to Yeager's plaint, took a look at the shoes of his mount, then made his proposition.

"This horse needs shoes all around. Me, I got a couple of broncs of my own that been runnin' barefoot too long. Tell you what, Hugh, we tackle this chore together, get all three animals took care of, I won't charge a cent for use of my forge and tools, or for a new set of shoes, either."

Yeager eyed him with a wry amusement. "Not a cent, eh Pete? Just a bucket of sweat. Well, if you can stand it, I can. Let's get busy."

Once well into the chore, Yeager found himself enjoying it, in spite of the copious sweat he'd prophesied. For in favor of some kind of physical release a man could shed mental problems and tensions. While Pete pumped the bellows steadily and the forge fire glowed white hot, Yeager donned the heavy leather farrier's apron and bent to the job, paring and rasping off excess hoof material, heating and working iron shoes to shape and fit before nailing them soundly in place. Along with the smell of coal smoke and the sweet, sour stench of scorched hoof was the steam that lifted when a hot shoe was plunged hissing into the cooling tub. All of these things he found pleasant in their peaceful earthiness.

So the morning hours slid away and it was full midday by the time the last shoe was in place and

Yeager able to wash up and sluice the sweat from his face and head. Drying himself on his shirttail he grinned at Pete Piett.

"You ought to be dealing faro somewhere, Pete. You'd make a fortune."

Pete grinned back. "You should thank me. That job did you good. There was a tight look about you when we started. It's gone now."

Yeager turned thoughtful again. "Understand Joe Hazle left town early this morning. He take one of your horses?"

"That big Idaho bronc he always uses. What about it?"

"He sent me word to meet him about this time of day."

"Well, he ain't back yet," Pete said. "Else he'd have turned the bay in."

Yeager rode uptown, tied at the marshal's office and went in. Somehow it seemed ominously still, with no recent hint of tobacco smoke to tell of occupancy. A desk drawer stood half open. Yeager wondered about that, and about the man in the jail, too. He went along the hall to see why the overall silence and atmosphere of emptiness was so complete. And he found out. The jail door was open, the key still in the lock. Ed Cruze, erstwhile prisoner, was gone. . . .

Swiftly back at the hotel, Yeager found Andy Stent in the kitchen, grumbling as he put another tray of food together.

"Didn't know I'd have to run this errand

twice. Wish Joe Hazle'd get back to feed his own prisoner."

"You can forget the food, Andy," Yeager said briefly. "There is no prisoner. He's gone."

"Gone?" Andy stared. "What do you mean, gone?"

"Just that. The jail's empty, the door open, the key still in the lock. Did you forget and leave it that way this morning?"

Andy exploded. "Hell no! I never unlocked no door. There's room under the door to slide a tray through, which is what I did. When I left, that feller was safe inside and the door was locked. If it ain't now, somebody else did it."

"Somebody else did," Yeager agreed.

"Sonofagun!" Andy mumbled. "Joe Hazle will be real upset!"

And with reason, reflected Yeager, returning to the street. Ed Cruze had been freed, he reasoned, while he and Pete Piett were at the chore of shoeing horses. Morning hours were generally slow ones in Piegan Junction, with few people on the street. Yet, someone might have noticed something. He carried this thought into the store and laid it before Duff Tealander. No, Duff hadn't seen a thing being busy all morning sorting and shelving supplies. But how about Mike Breedon . . . ?

Yeager went out and was about to cut over to the Lucky Seven when Station Agent Fred Glenn came out of the alley, climbed to the loading platform and dropped casual greeting.

"Howdy, Hugh! How are things?"

"Be better if I knew how a prisoner got out of Joe Hazle's jail this morning," Yeager told him. "You notice any strangers around, Fred?"

Fred Glenn laughed. "In a whistle-stop town like this, a railroad station can be the lonesomest place on earth. Which is why I'm here after tobacco. Nobody came by I could bum a smoke from."

He turned into the store and Yeager again started for the Lucky Seven but paused when Glenn came quickly back into sight.

"Just a minute, Hugh. Now you mention it, I did see something just before Twenty-nine came through at eight forty-five. A rider came out of the desert, leading a saddled horse, and cut around the lower end of the cattle pens. Pretty soon he rode back across the tracks and this time there was another fellow with him. They were headed toward that Big Sandy wash. It didn't strike me as queer at the time — but — there it is . . . !"

"And that's it!" Yeager exclaimed. "Obliged, Fred."

Up on his freshly shod horse, Yeager rode down past the cattle pens and swung across the railroad tracks. He found the trail without trouble for the hoof sign was plain, and he followed it to Big Sandy. Here he hauled up, eyes narrowed against the glare of this arid, alkali-whitened stretch of sand.

It was plain that the two riders had dropped

into the wash, but which way did they turn after that? If a man held to the bottom of the wash he might ride for miles, completely hidden from town. Putting his mount down into the wash, Yeager presently saw by the suddenly deep hoof gouges that one of the riders had made a plunging run for a break in the far bank. But now came a third set of hoof marks, also deeply cut, curving in from where a lone, heat-raveled cottonwood tree stood, then curving away again.

He saw more, a ragged furrow in the sand where something had been dragged. He followed this, hauling up once to study what lay in that furrow, caught and held and half-buried in the sand. A strip of torn calico, part of a man's shirt.

Out there in Big Sandy wash the sun was hot, but now a thread of chill touched Hugh Yeager's spine and his face became winter bleak as he followed the sign in the sand to where, close against the base of the cutbank, a portion of it had been broken down into a long, narrow mound.

Standing in his stirrups, Yeager looked up and down the wash, found it empty of all life. He stepped from his saddle and kicked aside some of the mounded dirt. When, presumably, boot leather struck against boot leather, he knew all he needed to know.

Back at town, he stopped by Joe Hazle's office, hoping the marshal had returned. The place was still empty so he rode down to the livery barn where Pete Piett snored sound asleep on a gunnysack bunk at the far end of the runway. Pete came reluctantly awake, complaining crankily when Yeager shook his shoulder.

"What now? What chore this time?"

"A mean one," Yeager told him. "Pete, there's a dead man out in Big Sandy wash. We're going after him. We'll need a wagon."

Coming thoroughly awake, Pete sputtered. "Another one? Godamighty! Be damned — another one. Between you and Joe Hazle! Who is it this time? Who killed him?"

"At a guess, the dead man is Ed Cruze. And the one who would profit most by the fact is Fletch Irby!"

It was Ed Cruze, all right. And when they got him cleared and into the back of the wagon and saw enough to understand the manner of his death, they were sickened as they drove slowly back to town and into the stable runway. Here they laid Cruze out and covered him with a blanket.

As they finished, another wagon came downstreet and turned into the stable runway. It was Soddy Neff, back from his repair job at the Sheridan Bench headquarters. Soddy was jumping with excitement and when he recognized Yeager in the warm shadows, he exclaimed eagerly.

"Was hopin' I'd locate you, Hugh. Because there's hell to pay at that ranch of yours on the Bench."

Yeager came quickly around. "How's that, Soddy?"

152

"For one thing, there was a shootin'," Soddy said. "Sam Carlock located some feller layin' out with a Winchester under that hawk's nest pine tree back of the ranch house, like he was waitin' a chance to dry-gulch somebody. Sam took that old buffalo gun of Buck Abbott's and snuck up on the feller. Sam gave him a chance to knuckle under, but the feller wouldn't listen. He tried to shoot it out, but Sam got there first!"

"Who was the man?" Yeager rapped.

"Sam named him Frenchy somethin'."

"Frenchy Dubois, of course," Yeager said harshly. "Out to make a second try. I'll have to give Sam a raise for that."

"The shootin' ain't all," Soddy added quickly. "One of your riders showed at the ranch just as I was fixin' to leave. He said a sizable jag of Sheridan Bench cattle had been pushed over Massacre Pass — mebbe as many as fifty head. Sometime last night by the sign. He said him and your other riders would be waiting for you along the Pass Road."

"Fair enough, and obliged, Soddy," Yeager said shortly. "Pete, you heard the word. When Joe Hazle returns, you tell it to him — about Ed Cruze, Frenchy Dubois — everything. And tell him I'll hunt him up later."

He was quickly gone then, stepping into his saddle and leaving town at a run.

Out at the lower ranch headquarters, things were quiet now. Fletch Irby and Whitey Mendell

153

had returned and while Whitey unsaddled the horses, Fletch Irby made his solid, heel-jarring way into the ranch house, alone with his thoughts. Reaction to the Big Sandy wash affair was at work. Not that he was regretting any part of it; he was too callous and frankly brutal for that. As he saw it, Ed Cruze was a squealer and rated no better than he got. But if Cruze had been persuaded to talk, then a certain Jeff Lord might also. There was only one way to make certain that he didn't.

Heavy-footed, heavy-handed, heavy-minded though he might have been in some things, Fletch Irby still owned a certain native shrewdness over what would or would not get real action from Sheriff Haley Lockyear's office in Empire City. This particular stretch of range was remote, unruly country with more than a sprinkle of wild ones riding through it — too many of such to keep real track of. So Lockyear was never overly concerned by a killing among the wild ones. In fact, he'd once stated he figured it smart to let the folks in the far back limits of the county "skin their own snakes."

Which, reasoned Irby, was one side of the card — the safe side. However, a witness like Ed Cruze or Jeff Lord, able to testify in court of a holdup attempt at big ranch money — even though it was not successful — could get things really moving in Lockyear's office and make things damned uncomfortable.

Even the fact that he'd worked Joe Hazle over

154

as he had did not worry Irby particularly. This, he felt, could be explained away as, while Hazle had claimed to be a resident deputy, he himself had read no official proof of this. And a town marshal, once beyond the limits of town, carried no more weight than anybody else. So, if he tried to throw his weight around and make an illegal arrest, then he had to take the consequences.

Right now what he had to do was locate this Jeff Lord hombre. Where to look for him? Most likely somewhere in the wild wilderness over across the Shoshone. Maybe at Elkhorn Flat. Maybe at Mack Snell's place on South Fork, or at Jack Cardinal's hangout. One of the three of them, Gabe Norton, Cardinal or Snell, should be able to put him on the trail of Jeff Lord. After that — well . . . !

From the back door of the ranch house Irby lifted a heavy call to Whitey Mendell.

"Put my saddle on a fresh bronc!"

When Whitey brought the horse, Irby tried the cinch, found it tight enough, then swung up.

"I may not be back before sometime tomorrow. So stick around close. Don't let anybody move in here. I mean — anybody!"

"How about him in there?" Whitey nodded toward the bunkhouse. "The one with the star?"

"Keep him right where he is," Irby ordered heavily. "Him and me, we'll have a little understanding before I turn him loose."

Whitey Mendell watched Fletch Irby swing past the corrals, strike the first lift of the hills at an angle and slant toward the distant, mist-blued summit. And as Irby's figure diminished in the distance, Whitey's lips curled and his pale eyes glinted with mockery. There was no real good in Whitey Mendell, never had been, never would be. He was all outlaw, ready to turn any crooked trick if there was money enough in it and the risk to his own skin was not too great. Now he was murmuring.

"Not for me, Mister Irby! I've seen enough of this particular trail and it's not for me. You're rough all right, and you're tough. And maybe you got the guts of a grizzly, but for the same reason that you don't know any better. It's in your mind that you're big enough to knock a mountain down, but I don't see you that size. A man could easy get killed, hanging around with you, and me — I don't figure to be one of them!"

Another member of Irby's jackleg crew came over from the bunkhouse.

"What now, Whitey? Why don't Irby lay something definite on the line? Here we are, but what do we do?"

"Stick around," Whitey said. "That's all, just stick around until he gets back some time tomorrow. Past that, Chink — I don't know what's on his mind. You worried?"

"Just wondering," Chink reported. "So's the rest of the boys. They ain't happy holding on to that feller Irby beat up. That man carries a star, Whitey. And it ain't never good, treating a star

156

packer that way. The boys don't like it and I don't like it."

"Neither do I," nodded Whitey. "Get the men out here. I got something to tell them."

They were a shifty-eyed, nondescript outfit of the same breed as Whitey, just as wild and unsettled, with plenty of shadows along their back trails, and just as predatory if the money and the odds were right. They had been lounging, sleeping, playing a little poker and becoming increasingly restless and uncertain. Whitey looked them over, then made his statement.

"When Fletch Irby got hold of me and offered me this job, I knew damn well he was just hiring me for my gun. I guess the same goes for the rest of you. Which is all right as that's our business to fight on one side or the other. But I draw the line on fighting the way Irby does. When men like us try it, they always lose. Fletch Irby don't care that for any one of us!" Whitey snapped his fingers.

"Me," he went on, "I'm pulling out. Irby's gone now. When he gets back, I won't be here. Rest of you can do as you please, but I'm leaving. I'll tell you why. Along with me you saw Irby beat that lawman half to death — maybe he would have killed him with his fists if I hadn't stepped in. Well, today I saw Fletch Irby do something worse than that. Out in the desert the other side of Piegan Junction, I saw him dab a loop around a man's neck and drag him to death. He wanted to shut that man's mouth over some

157

deal he'd used him on, and by the way Irby acted he enjoyed doing it that way. But me — while I got a rind on me as thick as most, I sure as hell didn't enjoy it! There's a crazy streak in Fletch Irby. He's too wild and rough for me. So I'm hauling out."

A stir ran through Whitey's listeners. One of them said: "That's pretty rough, all right — draggin' a man to death. If Irby's too rough for you, Whitey, the same goes for me."

"And here," said Chink. "I hit this place with nothin' so I can leave with nothin'. Rest of you better come along."

Whitey's roving glance saw that there were no dissenters. "We turn that lawman loose," he said. "We put him on his horse and wish him well. We show him we expected no part of a deal like this and that we want no part of it. How's that sound?"

"Smart!" said Chink.

There were no dissenters to this so they saddled and brought around Joe Hazle's horse. They helped him out of the bunkhouse and into his saddle. He was still shaky and badly used up and his battered face pulled thin in a grimace of pain as he reared straight in his saddle.

"Where's Fletch Irby?" he demanded sternly.

"Headed out," explained Whitey Mendell. "Won't be back until sometime tomorrow, so he said. Rest of us are leaving, too — and we won't be back. We hired blind into something that listened all right but didn't pan out that way. We want no quarrel with you."

"Maybe you don't," Joe Hazle said, harsh and direct. "But you'll have one, should I ever meet up with any of you again. You better remember that and ride far!"

He reined away then, sitting straight up and grim-jawed until he felt he was well beyond their view. Then his shoulders sagged and he hunched over, a weary, sick viciously beaten man, stoically facing the long miles to town.

X

Putting his horse steadily to the lift of the Sheridan Bench grade, Hugh Yeager carried thoughts that were dark and somber. Because to date, he'd handled his assumed stewardship of Lorie Anselm's ranch affairs any way but smartly. And done little better with his own, for that matter. So far, Fletch Irby had outmaneuvered him completely, being right now in full control of the lower ranch. While someone, Jack Cardinal probably, had made a heavy raid on the Sheridan Bench herd. If Cardinal and Irby should be working together, which seemed likely, they would whipsaw him to rags unless brought to a damn stern halt — and quickly.

If any final proof was needed to prove that in Fletch Irby he was up against a cruel and ruthless savage, the cold-blooded killing of Ed Cruze supplied it. In his way Jack Cardinal was little better. Though he might not kill with the vengeful ferocity Irby had shown, Cardinal was still all sly, tricky thief, and there was no middle ground on which to deal with either of them. It was now a simple question of stark survival. You eliminated them or they eliminated you. This was the bleak conviction Yeager carried with him into the hills.

He found his four man crew waiting where the main north-south Bench trail crossed the Massacre Pass Road. By now the afternoon was running out; the sun was far over and smoke blue shadows were flowing thinly through the timber. The still air was heavy with a baked out essence of resin. The crew showed relief at his arrival and Miles Grayson, oldest of them, gave him the word with a laconic brevity.

"Some time last night Cardinal and his crowd took a heavy bite out of us, Hugh. I say Cardinal because I know of no one else with enough men to make so big a gather at night in this kind of country and then push it over the pass. I'd guess that at least fifty head of our beef stock that yesterday were living fat and easy in these timber meadows, are now across the summit. We going after them?"

Yeager would have liked nothing better than to be able to say "yes," as the banked, frustrated anger in him made him hungry to hit back. But this crew of his was much too small to face an all out smoke-rolling showdown against the present odds either Irby or Cardinal could muster. Besides which, this was his fight not theirs. The cards in this affair had been dealt directly to him, and whatever their worth, it was up to him to play them the best he knew how. So he shook his head.

"Not now, Miles. Fletch Irby is dug in at the

lower ranch. We can't chance him gaining the same edge up here. If he did we'd be just a bunch of strays, siwashing it in the hills with no place to light. We can afford to lose some cattle and still be in shape to fight back. But we can't afford to lose our home headquarters. That's one fort we got to hold!"

Grayson grinned faintly. "Sam Carlock did a fair job at that today by himself. You know about Frenchy Dubois?"

"Soddy Neff told me," Yeager nodded. "Missing his chance to gulch me at the lower ranch, Frenchy must have figured on a second try. The man was a backbiting, cowardly dog. I should have gunned him that day when I had him dead to rights. If I had, Ben Hardisty might still be alive. I'm glad Sam got Dubois. May I do as well with Fletch Irby next time I meet up with him!"

"Ah!" murmured Grayson. "So it's come to that, has it?"

"Yes," Yeager said. "It's come to that. Now let's get along home."

The sun was fully down when they arrived and Sam Carlock had the house lights glowing yellow through the early dusk. He stuck his head from the door to identify them as they rode up, then beat out the supper summons on an iron triangle.

"Grub's ready," he announced when they trooped in. "Figured some of you were due to show, so had things simmering."

They ate hungrily and Yeager, glancing along the table, was again struck with the depth of his responsibility toward these men. Like, for instance, young Johnny Richert. The kid, Yeager knew, would follow him through hell fire should he say the word. But given any luck at all, Johnny had a lot of long and good years ahead of him which no man had the moral right to jeopardize. Then there was that inseparable brother team, Abe and Danny Lancaster. Should a hostile gun slug ever break up that team, the survivor would be a lonely, stricken soul throughout all the rest of his days.

With Miles Grayson it might be different, Yeager mused. So far as he knew Grayson had no kin. Outwardly he was a mild, easygoing sort, but this appearance cloaked a steel wire inner toughness and a readiness to face any odds at any time in defense of what he believed in. And in a tight corner no man could ask for a better partner to back his hand.

As for Sam Carlock, he was just old Sam Carlock, kind enough to sit up all night nursing a sick chipmunk, but tough enough to kill in a situation where killing was necessary.

These were his troops as Yeager saw them. Too few and too valuable to risk beyond reason. So, until and unless some inescapable showdown was forced upon him, he'd continue to try and fight through on this thing with cool reason and thought. Like following up on the angle that brought about the cruel death of Ed Cruze. The fact that Fletch Irby was willing to chance a thing of that sort showed how wary he was of being brought to face a court of law. There was in back of that act a certain desperation.

Done with food, Yeager pushed back his chair and built a smoke. "Got to see Joe Hazle about something, so I'm off for town again. Rest of you stick close. Miles, you're in charge." He turned to Sam Carlock. "How was it with Frenchy Dubois, Sam?"

Soberly, old Sam told it as it had been. Ending, he said: "I gave him full chance to ear down peaceful, Hugh. He wouldn't listen. His rifle is on the rack now with the buffalo Sharps. It's a Winchester .38-56. I had no choice."

"You did damn well," Yeager told him. "So don't let it bother you."

"Bother me? Not a chance," Sam declared. "I'm too old and sinful to lose sleep over a no good hombre like Frenchy Dubois."

When Yeager broke from the timber and began the downward slant to the desert flats, the moon, nearing full, hung big and round over the hills. Through the flood of its silver white glow, the distant lights of Piegan Junction seemed pressed down and subdued. Still carrying some of the past day's dwindling warmth, the desert air moved up the hill slope, dry and bittersweet with the breath of distance.

In town, Joe Hazle's office was still dark and empty, so Yeager went along to the store where lights burned. Here he found Duff Tealander and Frank Cornelius, and there was a sober gravity in both of them as they came around to face him.

"Joe Hazle — where the hell is he?" Yeager questioned. "He sent word I was to meet him in town around noon today. He wasn't there then, and from the looks of his office he's not here now."

"He's in town, Hugh," said Frank Cornelius quietly. "In his bed in the hotel, about as badly used up as a man could be and still stay alive after being mauled by a God damned animal. Face all clubbed out of shape and some ribs caved in. Helen Stent and Lorie Anselm have done a fair job of caring for him so far, but I had Fred Glenn use the railroad wire to Empire City for a doctor, who should be in on the next train. Joe's been asking for you. You better get along and see him."

"Right away," Yeager said, turning for the door. "You heard about Ed Cruze, of course?"

"Also, about Frenchy Dubois. Soddy Neff gave us that word. And you can blame Fletch Irby for both." Cornelius shook his head. "Did I say a damned animal . . . !"

In the hotel, the first person Yeager saw was Lorie Anselm. She was carrying a basin of hot water, and she looked at him with stricken eyes from a pale and tired face. When Yeager asked for Joe Hazle she tipped her head. "This way."

Helen Stent was in the room, waiting. She

dipped a towel in the hot water, wrung it out and spread it carefully over a man's bruised and swollen face. Yeager stood beside the bed.

"Hugh Yeager here, Joe," he said. "Anything you want to tell me?"

Answer came slow and muffled through the folds of the steaming towel.

"You're looking at the world's biggest damn fool, Hugh. Against Irby I played my hand like a raw, bald-faced kid. When I braced him, I figured the star I carried was all the weight I needed. It wasn't — not near. He grabbed me, hauled me out of the saddle and went at me like a mad bear. He came down on me with his bunched knees and I felt my ribs cave. He near beat my head off with his fists. And he laughed and bragged that Ed Cruze would never testify against him in any court. He made sure of that, I understand, by dragging the poor devil to death. Hugh, from now on I live for just one thing — a chance to face Irby again. When I do, if he so much as moves a finger he's dead!"

Mounting feeling deepened the marshal's tone and Helen Stent looked at Yeager meaningly. Understanding, he nodded.

"Don't fret, Joe," he comforted. "Friend Irby's getting into deeper water all the time. First thing he knows, he'll be in over his head."

"Could be there already," declared Hazle. "That hard case crew he had rounded up — well, they're gone. Irby doesn't know that. He wasn't there when they turned me loose and pulled out saying they didn't like the way things were shaping up. But I played my hand so damned stupid," the marshal went on lamenting. "If I'd kept my mouth shut Irby wouldn't have known I had Cruze locked up. I'd even left the jail keys in a desk drawer where they were easy found. Man, I got a lot to make up for."

"Not a thing, not a thing," Yeager differed. "Take it easy and get back on your feet. I'll be around, Joe."

When he left the room Lorie Anselm went with him, then faced him with a near tearful defiance.

"This has done it, Hugh. I'm not waiting any longer. Fletch Irby can have the ranch — any of it or all of it. It should have been that way to begin with. And because it wasn't, Ben Hardisty is dead. Now that poor, helpless prisoner dead too — dragged to death!" She shuddered. "How horrible! Nothing is worth such things — no ranch — anything. I'm going to get hold of Fletch Irby and tell him he can have my share for nothing; just so he'll quit this, this killing . . . !"

Yeager did not try and argue with her. She was too emotionally upset to respond to logic just now. She was reasoning with her heart not her head. Reaching for time, he spoke as if about to agree with her.

"You could be right, Lorie. But suppose you let me hunt up Fletch Irby and speak to him about it. I don't know where he is just now, but I'll locate him."

167

She did not answer to this, standing with her head bent, and from the way her throat was working, fighting to hold back the tears. Then also, in the way she stood and the way she held her head there was the suggestion of a forlorn loneliness. And these things tore him up inside. So he tucked a finger under her chin and brought her head up. The tears were there all right, flooding her eyes with a sort of blind loveliness as she looked at him.

"That's better, Lorie," he said, gruffly gentle. "Remember, I'm here. I'll always be here. You're not alone."

It was then that she came close to him, well into the circle of his arm, her head burrowing against his shoulder. And when a little later, the tears ceased and she again looked up at him trying to smile, he bent and stilled the soft trembling of her lips with the press of his own.

It was not a consciously thought out thing. It just happened was all, and it was the most tremendously real thing he had ever known. The warm, sweet heat and shock of it reached all the way to his heels. And when presently they moved apart regarding each other with a sort of startled wonder, it was Yeager who recovered first.

"I didn't plan that," he said carefully. "But I meant it, Lorie — I sure meant it . . . !"

He watched her eyes clear and widen and fill with a soft confusion.

"Hugh!" she whispered. "Oh Hugh . . . !"

She turned then and scurried away.

Yeager took his surging emotions and tumbling thoughts out into the night and from the lift of the hotel porch surveyed the street shining whitely in the moonlight. Aside from the one occupied by his own mount, the hitch rails of the town stood empty. As he pondered this fact, a rider turned in at the upper end of the street and came along it so slowly the move brought down Yeager's hard attention. Most generally, thirsty and impatient, riders hit town at a run. But the approach of this one verged on the furtive and Yeager eased deeper into the shadow of the porch overhang, still and watchful.

Once the rider pulled completely to a halt, as though to more thoroughly test the silent emptiness of the street and decide on the cause. He finally ended his cautious approach at the Lucky Seven where he eased from his saddle and stood for another small interval close to his horse, sheltered by the bulk of the animal. When he finally made for the door of the Lucky Seven, he moved quickly.

For the brief moment as the door opened to let the man through, Yeager had him against the light in partial profile and knew immediate conviction of having seen him before. The distance was too great and the time too short to get things in detail, but there was something in the shape of the shoulders and the way the head was carried that registered, so Yeager dropped quickly to the street and moved in on the saloon.

He was set and ready as he pushed open the door of the place and knew no particular surprise when the roan head and hard, pale eyes of Bruno Orr swung his way. Bruno Orr, segundo of Jack Cardinal's outfit, facing Mike Breedon across the bar. Yeager dropped in beside him.

"Well now, this is a surprise. Kind of late to be showing up, Orr. What brings you to town?"

Plainly wary and uneasy, Orr tipped a shoulder. "Just happened to be down this way. Thought I'd take on a drink before heading home. Have one with me?"

Mike Breedon had already set out a bottle and glass. He looked the question at Yeager, who laughed softly and shook his head.

"No thanks, all around. Against my principles to drink with them who steal my cattle."

As he spoke he moved with a smooth, sure speed, and then the muzzle of his gun was against Bruno Orr's ribs. Startled and beginning to turn, Orr froze.

"Smart!" Yeager approved, lifting the rustler's gun. He tossed this over the bar, then nodded toward the whiskey bottle. "Go ahead, Bruno — have your drink. Then we'll go."

"Go! Go where?" Orr stared sullenly before appealing to Breedon. "Mike — you standing for this? Can't a man be peaceful at your bar without having a gun shoved in his ribs?"

"Mike hasn't a damn thing to say about it," remarked Yeager dryly. "If he didn't know before that you were a damned cow thief, he knows it now. How about that, Mike?"

Breedon spread both hands on the bar top, palms down. "Whatever this is, it's between you two. I want no part of it, nohow!"

"You see, Bruno," murmured Yeager. "It's like I said. So have your drink, pay the man, and we'll be on our way."

Bruno Orr went stubborn, shaking his narrow roan head. "Hell with you! I'm staying right here. You don't bluff me."

Yeager grinned wickedly. "Bruno," he said smoothly, "you're making a mistake. Because this is no bluff. I quit bluffing some time ago. Oh, I admit I wouldn't enjoy pulling the trigger of this gun and messing up Mike's floor — but there is always this!"

He flicked his gun through a short, chopping arc, laying the barrel of it across Orr's head. The rustler grunted, sagged against the bar and slid down. Now Mike Breedon did growl mild complaint.

"Cow thief or no cow thief — was that necessary?"

"I figured so," Yeager told him shortly. "Maybe you better listen, Mike, instead of talking. Last night Jack Cardinal and his crowd got away with fifty head of my beef stock. This fellow is Cardinal's right hand man so he was bound to be along on the raid. Well, together with many other things, that's the way it is in these parts. Rough, Mike — rough as hell. So from here on out, I handle Orr and others like him the way they deserve. Let's have your water bucket!"

Breedon offered no further argument. Yeager splashed Orr's head and face, saw his eyes presently flutter and open.

"On your feet," Yeager ordered harshly. "Pour him his drink, Mike. Make it a big one."

It took a second dousing from the water bucket before Bruno Orr climbed groggily to his feet. He didn't hesitate over the whiskey, emptying the glass in a couple of greedy gulps. Yeager tossed a coin on the bar.

"My treat. Now we go." He took Orr by the arm.

The rustler shambled along, sullen but obedient. Outside Yeager collected Orr's horse and led it to where his own waited. Here he took his riata, dropped the loop over Orr's head, pulled it snug and threw a knot against the honda to keep it that way.

"This," he said conversationally, "is how we go home, Orr. Should you get reckless along the way, it will be your neck. You know, earlier today Fletch Irby put his rope around a man's neck and dragged him to death. Must have been one hell of a tough way for a man to die, don't you think? Well . . . ?"

Bruno Orr said nothing; the game was running too fast against him. He climbed into his saddle and led the way out of town, on across the desert flats to the foot of the hill slope, then up it. They met no one along the way; the world, chilling now as they climbed, belonged entirely to them and the creatures of the night. Back in the timber, a horned owl set up its hollow booming and later, from some high and distant point, a timber wolf bayed the moon, hoarse and wild.

Aside from a curt order of direction now and then, Yeager kept his silence also. When they rode in at headquarters, everything lay dark and still until the voice of Miles Grayson came forward in brief challenge.

"Hugh?"

"Right."

"Who else?"

"An old acquaintance — Mister Bruno Orr."

Grayson's exclamation was sharp. "Hell you say! How'd it happen?"

"Met him in town. Got plans for him. What are you nighthawking for?"

"Just get that way when the moon's too bright for sleeping."

Stepping from his saddle, Yeager spoke meaningly. "We still got company in the saddle shed, Miles?"

An alert man, Grayson got it instantly. "Still there," he said. "Can't move him out until daylight tomorrow. Why?"

"Thought I'd let friend Bruno have a look," Yeager said. "Might loosen up his thinking."

"I'll get a lantern," Grayson said.

By the light of this they led Bruno Orr into the saddle shed, where something lay, covered with a blanket. Miles Grayson lifted one end of the blanket. Bruno Orr gulped and stared.

"Frenchy Dubois! He's — dead . . . ?"

"As he'll ever be," returned Yeager bleakly. "He bet on the wrong horse, Orr. Figured Fletch Irby had the makings of a brand new god and that hombres like you and Jack Cardinal just couldn't miss this time around. Also with ideas about gulching folks and all that sort of slimy business. You see how wrong he was. You could have made the same mistake. What do you think?"

At the moment Bruno Orr wasn't thinking very well. This was the camp of the enemy, and he was in it with a rope around his neck and facing the dread mockery of that dead man under the blanket.

"You — you lynched him . . . ?"

"Not exactly. Yet you notice the end result is the same," laid on Yeager remorselessly. "But a lynch rope is the oldest and best known remedy to cure a cow thief, and if that's the way you want it that's the way you'll get it. Unless you open up and do a little talking. You sneaked into town tonight like a calf-killing coyote. Why?"

Orr offered no argument nor did he try and hedge the point. He was past all that and was the sort, once he started to retreat, to keep on backing away.

"Cardinal sent me," he blurted. "To sort of look around."

"Of course," nodded Yeager sarcastically. "To see if the goose was still fat and stupid and ripe for another picking. That it?"

Orr shrugged. "Close enough."

174

"Maybe Cardinal has another raid in mind?"

At this, Orr hesitated. Watching, Miles Grayson again twitched the blanket aside. "Want another look, Bruno?"

"And," reminded Yeager gently, "consider a high tree and a strong rope for a cow thief. Which all honest men will approve. Another raid, Bruno . . . ?"

"Yeah," said Orr hoarsely. "Tomorrow night. To pull you south along the Bench range while Fletch Irby moves in and takes over here."

Yeager exclaimed. "Ah! Like I reasoned. Irby and Cardinal — working together."

"Have been," Orr said, "ever since Buck Abbott kicked off. They were figuring this deal when I left Elkhorn Flat."

"When were you to report back to Cardinal?"

"That would depend. Long as everything was quiet and the trails clear, I was to hang around in these parts and meet him and the rest of the boys tomorrow night when they came over the pass. Only if things didn't look good was I to head home earlier and warn him off."

"And Irby is at Elkhorn Flat?"

"Was when I left. Him and Cardinal and Mack Snell were at Gabe Norton's place lining things up. But I did hear Irby say he was heading back to the lower ranch later tonight."

Again Yeager exclaimed softly, "That's good, that's what I want. Miles, catch me up a fresh horse, then keep an eye on friend Bruno here until I get back."

175

"He'll be here," Grayson promised. "But where you going?"

"The lower ranch. I want to be there when Irby arrives."

Grayson's protest was quick. "You off your head? Irby's got a whole crew of rough ones there. Abe Lancaster told you that."

"Irby thinks he has a crew. The one he had pulled out not wanting to buck the law. Joe Hazle gave me that word. I've been hoping for this chance. Just Fletch Irby and me!"

Miles Grayson still protested. "I don't like it, Hugh. Sure, you're a hell of a lot of man in a hell of a lot of ways — but you're no gunslinger. Man to man and no guns, I'd bet on you, even if Irby is a wild bull. But if a smoke-rolling shapes up — you better have me along."

Yeager swung his shoulders impatiently. "Some other time, Miles — not this one. I've never made any pretense of being a gunslinger, but I can come up a notch or two with a .44 when I have to. Go get that horse!"

Grayson brought the horse, saddled it, and offered one final question.

"No deal of this sort is ever a sure thing bet. So if you don't come back — what then, Hugh?"

"Write your own ticket," Yeager told him.

XI

Heading northwest, Hugh Yeager aimed to come off the end of the Sheridan Bench somewhat beyond the lower ranch headquarters. He pushed his horse steadily, lifting it to a run when open ground lay ahead, keeping it at a driving trot through the timber, riding low and tight in the saddle, dodging heavy limbs, warding off lighter ones with thrusting arms and swinging shoulders. And while the moonlight helped greatly, it also seemed a man owned an instinct at finding the clearer way. Or perhaps the credit belonged to the strong, surefooted horse under him. Whatever the reason, he made good time which was what he planned; to be at the headquarters when Fletch Irby rode in and so have the element of surprise on his side.

He came out of the timber and down to the flats a good half mile beyond the headquarters, which put him on its blind side. Now, as the full impact of the possibilities of this thing struck home, he slowed his horse to a walk. After all, he was acting purely on hearsay, and how much of that could be taken at its face value?

Joe Hazle claimed Irby's hard case crew had

pulled out. Had they really, or merely given Joe that impression to muddy up the waters? Again, how much that Bruno Orr admitted could be believed? No question but that Orr was a badly shaken individual when he looked at the dead face of Frenchy Dubois, and if there was any truth in him at all, such an experience could shake it loose. Too, what he had told was credible because it was logical. So, Yeager mused, you listened to these things and acted on them because they led to something you felt you had to do.

He hauled up, surveying the bulk of the ranch buildings ahead. They stood dark and silent, no glimmer of light or thread of sound anywhere. So far so good. Right or wrong, acting on truth or lies, he'd come too far and with too much at stake to back away now. Thinking on this, on why he was here and what he intended to do, gave him the strange feeling that he was viewing these things from some point of remote objectivity.

It did no good to beg the question in any way. He was here this night to probably kill a man. It was that simple though, of course, such a prospect was not a simple thing and never would be. There was no use to call it impersonal because it was so strongly personal. There were two ways by which you could accomplish such an act. You could copy the way of Frenchy Dubois, which was to get your man from ambush, and shoot him in the back. Stripped of all theories of right or wrong, that was the entirely safe way, the efficient and sure way. But it was also the murder way — the dirty murder way. And after it a man would have a hell of a time trying to live with himself. Yet, if you deliberately set out to kill a man, even in a face to face, fair shake showdown, did that make it any more legitimate . . . ?

Yeager scrubbed a tired hand across his face. It had been one hell of a long day, a wearisome day charged with revelations that exhausted a man emotionally as well as physically. Perhaps, he decided somberly, he was anticipating punishment where there would be none. He'd already had one man go down before him, that one in Tealander's alley, the night of his return from Omaha. He'd certainly killed there and had lost no sleep over it. Maybe, as was the case on that occasion, if the other fellow was shooting at you, had already thrown the first shot, then if you killed him it made everything legitimate, with some inner wisdom telling you so and making it all right. Maybe there was a basic rightness to survival during any moment of stark need which could comfort and clear a man's conscience.

In considering the act, you had to consider the man too, and in this case that helped — mightily. Because over the short space of a few days, Fletch Irby had spread a savagery too brutal and ruthless to be reconciled under any circumstances. Directly or indirectly, he was responsible for the deaths of four men and the wicked beating of a fifth. While he lived, there would

179

certainly be more of the same.

There must have been, Yeager finally decided, some sort of mental catharsis supplied by these moments of sober reflection because, as he sent his horse forward, he felt better about things. A man did what he had to do. . . .

As he had done when he caught Frenchy Dubois off guard, Yeager left his horse well back and went in on foot. When he warily circled the cavvy corral he knew a lift of satisfaction. Joe Hazle had been right. There was no crew here else their horses would have been in this corral. Now the enclosure stood empty.

He moved faster and more surely. The bunkhouse held nothing but darkness and silence and the ranch house, when he crossed to it, was equally empty. Following the feeble glow of several matches, the only sign he found of recent habitation was a half-empty whiskey bottle and a glass on a table top, along with several discarded cigarette butts. But the whiskey glass was scummed and dry and the cigarette butts long cold and dead.

There was nothing to do now but wait this thing out.

Back across the hill summit it was well past midnight when Fletch Irby finally left Elkhorn Flat. His mood was surly, as things had not gone well at all. His search for Jeff Lord turned up empty; if he had been hanging out in this country, he was no longer there, so to make that quest good meant looking farther and somewhere else. This fact was only a part of the cause for his sour mood. Fletch Irby hated to lose at anything, and this night he had lost heavily at stud poker. Four of them had been in the game in Gabe Norton's deadfall. Gabe Norton, Jack Cardinal, Mack Snell and himself. The game had started after they finished their planning for the joint strike against Hugh Yeager.

Fletch Irby knew only one way to go at anything, which was violently. He played poker that way, glowering, dark-browed, heavy handed. He plainly hated any man who won a pot from him, and just as plainly knew contempt for the loser when it was the other way around. Nor did he bother to cover up either expression. There was no sense of fineness in him. When he ran a bluff he tried to make it stand by the sheer pressure of his dark feelings.

With some timid souls, these tactics might have worked. With the three who ringed the table across from him, they got him nowhere. With massive, fat-mounded shoulders hunched over his cards, Gabe Norton sat inscrutable and without expression no matter what the bet or its outcome. Jack Cardinal played much as he lived, with considerable rambling talk and short bursts of soundless laughter when he won a hand, which was particularly irritating to Irby. Mack Snell was a slight, rather small man, taciturn in mood and clipped of speech, with a metallic hardness in his black eyes that had made many a bigger man back up. All were experienced at the cards, and once they read Irby's method of play, proceeded to strip him down to empty pockets. When, with a curse of disgust, he finally pushed back his chair, Jack Cardinal looked at him with just the faintest hint of mockery.

"If you're shy of cash, Fletch, your I.O.U. is good with me. We got a lot of good-paying deals ahead of us."

"Hell with it!" Irby growled. "I'm heading out. We hit Yeager tomorrow night, remember."

"That's it," Cardinal nodded. "Just as we agreed."

Gabe Norton heaved ponderously to his feet, shuffled over to his bar. "Pour you a drink, Fletch. Keep the chill out going over the pass."

Irby put the drink away without a word of thanks, then stamped out and spurred away from the flat at a gallop. In the deadfall, Gabe Norton lifted a moist, breathy yell that presently brought his slattern woman with a jug of hot coffee.

"You win?" she asked greedily.

Norton grunted. "Enough," and tossed her a gold half eagle. "Go back to bed."

He poured coffee for himself and Cardinal and Mack Snell, then looked across his lifted cup at the other two.

"If Irby runs all his affairs like he plays stud poker, he's going nowhere, and neither are we if we tie in too tight with him."

"Just so," agreed Mack Snell curtly. "He's

182

dangerous to be around. Don't take him too much at face value, Jack."

Jack Cardinal gave out his silent laugh. "I take him at no value at all. We'll share the hand as long as he's useful. Then we'll close the door."

The chill was there, all right, going over the pass, and burly and insensitive as he was, Fletch Irby got the denim jumper from behind his saddle cantle and donned it. He knew nothing of the thoughts of those he left behind at Elkhorn Flat and didn't give a damn. That crowd might take him at poker, but in what really counted he'd win every hand. Once he'd used them to gain full control of both ends of the Double A ranch, then he'd hit that Elkhorn Flat country some dark night, and when he was through with it there wouldn't be a healthy cow thief left to ever bother his future. Which included that ungainly blob of fat, Gabe Norton, too, by God!

Across the pass and dropping fast, Irby made his angle cut for the desert flats; and when he reached them and lined out for the lower ranch, he rode through the breath of an approaching dawn. The moon was far down in the west, its light dimmed by a bank of haze. Tough as he was physically, Irby knew the drag of weariness, as did his horse, faltering slightly now in its stride. But he kept driving on, uncaring. With him, both horses and people were considered only to the extent they served his ends.

It had been a long, long night for Hugh

Yeager, too. Waiting through the slow, cold hours of midnight and the very early hours of morning had been a form of mild torture because he had to stay awake and reasonably alert. So he did a lot of walking, up and down, back and forth. He didn't dare lie down anywhere. Once he crouched on his heels, back against a ranch house wall. Sleep sneaked up on him like a thief in the night and he nearly toppled over. So again it was a case of back on his feet and keep moving.

A smoke would have helped mightily, but he couldn't chance it. He remembered how the taint of cigarette smoke had led him to Frenchy Dubois, and in the still, heavy night air the breath of a cigarette would hang on and on. So he looked at the night and he listened to the night and he moved about through the night with a stoic determination that had him still up and active when the first gray light of dawn seeped across the land. With it came what he'd been straining his ears for — the thump of nearing hoofs.

There was, at the corner of the ranch house, a pocket of shadow still deep enough to hide him fully. From this he watched the approach, caught the bulk of horse and rider against the growing light and knew that here at last was his man. Strangely enough after all the buildup of emotion and seesawing thoughts, there now came to him a sense of complete certainty and coolness. He would do what he had to do. . . .

Fletch Irby pulled his faltering mount to a stop and lifted a harsh call as he swung down.

"Mendell! Whitey Mendell! Send somebody out here to take care of this bronc. And get some breakfast going. What the hell's wrong with you? Here's daylight coming over the hills and all you lazy bastards still in your blankets. Come alive — come alive . . . !"

The call echoed and died among the empty ranch buildings. Irby blurted an angry curse and lunged for the bunkhouse. Watching, Yeager saw the yellow light of a kerosene lamp flicker, then build to a steady glow. The light continued to burn, but Fletch Irby came stumbling out, spilling his mumbled words of disbelief.

"Gone — they're gone. . . . Mendell — the rest — all of them gone, Joe Hazle gone, too. Why — where . . . ? What the hell is this?"

"It's payoff, Fletch," Yeager called. "Payoff catching up with you at last. It's Yeager here, Fletch — Hugh Yeager. You can drop your gun or try and use it . . . !"

He stepped into the clear as he spoke, measuring the distance and the burly figure at the end of it. Irby's exclamation of surprise was a feral growl as he whipped into action, whirling, half-crouching. The slap of his hand against the butt of his gun was a sharp echo, drowned out immediately by the hard smash of gun report.

Knowing Fletch Irby and his ways, Yeager had gambled on that first shot, gambled that under the spur of surprise and bewilderment it would be hurried and headlong and consequently not too true. In addition he would be moving as Irby moved, ready to use the small but definite interval of time it would take Irby to correct and get off a second try. If he guessed right, all would be well. If he didn't . . .

He guessed right. He heard the thud of Irby's slug against the ranch house wall beside him and now his own gun was leveled and steady and careful, and when it blared its report and bounced in recoil, he knew the shot was good. He heard Irby gasp under the shock of the big slug, heard the choked curse that followed. Yet Irby stayed on his feet, shooting again and again. But Yeager's slug had knocked all coordination and balance out of him, so his shots were wild and desperate. Again, and carefully, Yeager fired, and this time Irby went down, a last fading curse dribbling from his lips, a man dying as violently as he had lived.

Afterward, the silence ran so deep it was as if the whole world was listening for another word that never came.

Yeager went slowly forward to stand beside the huddled figure of Fletch Irby. Now that it was over with, it seemed that the weight of the entire universe had come down upon his shoulders. A pit of abysmal chill formed inside him, and something near to pure anguish deepened the bitterness in his murmured words.

"It didn't have to be this way. Buck Abbott left enough for all of us. A little more judgment — a

186

sense of justice — that would have done it. Instead this, this . . ."

There was no satisfaction, no lift of thankfulness because a long gamble had come off in his favor. Left was only a shocked and draining sadness. Because at one time Buck Abbott had known great plans for this man who now lay dead in the still, gray dawn.

But the timeless turning of the earth was not about to pause over any tragedy among mere men. So the dawn gave way to a glass clear light and the eastern sky beyond the Shoshones flushed with the approach of the sun. And because there were still many things to be done, some perhaps fully as violent as this had been, Yeager turned and went away after his horse.

The wailing whistle cry of the morning Overland signaling its approach carried across the desert as Yeager rode in at Piegan Junction. The train's halt was brief leaving off a stocky, gray-haired man with a voluminous black satchel. This lone passenger wended his way to the street and along it to the hotel.

"I'm Doctor Reese," he told Andy Stent. "You've an injured man here in need of medical attention?"

"Just so, Doctor," Andy assured. "Right this way."

Hauling up at the hotel hitch rail, Yeager saw the new arrival enter and guessed his errand. His own plan had been to report directly to Joe

Hazle, but now he'd have to wait until the doctor had finished. In the meantime, Lorie Anselm would have to be told, and he wondered dully what her reaction would be. How would a gentle soul look at a man fresh from slaughter . . . ?

He left his saddle stiffly and went on in, finding things empty all the way back to the kitchen, finding this room empty too at the moment. But there was coffee brewing on the big iron cooking range so he took a cup from a shelf, filled it from the steaming pot, then eased down into a chair beside the kitchen table savoring the first big drag of coffee. He was there, brooding, when a few moments later Helen Stent came in, exclaiming at sight of him.

"Hugh! What brings you here?"

"Some of this and some of that," he answered gravely. "Did I see a doctor arrive?"

"Yes, thank goodness! Lorie and I, we did the best we knew how for Joe Hazle, but he's been in considerable pain. Now he'll get proper care and some relief."

"If Lorie's handy, tell her I'm here," he requested.

Carrying hot water, Helen Stent hurried out. Yeager sagged deeper in his chair, weary to the last inch of his long, whalebone body. Still and all, the hot savor of the coffee brought back some feeling of normalcy. His cup was empty when Lorie Anselm came in. She knew at a glance something was wrong and crossed quickly to him.

"Hugh, what is it?"

He didn't look up as he told her. "Fletch Irby is dead, Lorie. He and I shot it out at the lower ranch. I killed him."

Underestimating the true depths of this girl's strength and character, he had thought the word might shock and repulse her. But the soft cry she gave was for him not herself, and moving close she put her arms about his head and pulled it against her.

"It's all right, Hugh — all right . . . !" she comforted. "All along I've felt something of that sort would happen. And it's all right . . . !"

He could hear the steady rhythm of her heart and her fragrance was all about him, and under the caress of these things the hard bitterness in him began to lessen. Presently she drew away and he looked up to meet the soft concern in her eyes. She spoke again with her swift, feminine wisdom.

"Poor man, you're completely beat out and hungry. Go wash up while I get you some breakfast."

Hot water and soap and a brisk toweling helped; these were some of the little things that tied a man to the practical business of everyday living. Hot savory food was another. He referred back to the morning's affair just once.

"I keep thinking about all the things Buck Abbott once hoped for Fletch Irby. If Buck was sitting in judgment now, what would he say?"

"That we'll never know," Lorie said gravely.

"But of one thing I'm sure. Uncle Buck wrote Fletch off the day he changed his will. I heard him say as much to Frank Cornelius and Duff Tealander. Whatever the future of the Double A ranches might be, they were turned over to you, Hugh — not to Fletch Irby."

Yeager thought about this for a time in silence. "Maybe," he said finally, "that's as good an answer as any. We'll leave it so."

It was midmorning before the doctor was done with Joe Hazle and Yeager was able to go in. Hazle showed him a wry, twisted grin.

"Now I know how a saddle bronc feels when the cinch is set. That doc, he's got me wrapped so tight I'm no bigger around than the belly of a sidewinder snake. But there's a comfort in it — a real comfort."

"Nothing worse than some bent ribs then?" Yeager said.

"Bent — hell!" retorted Hazle. "Busted, that's what. Fletch Irby is no lightweight and when he landed on me with bunched knees — well, something had to give. My ribs did. Like I said before, I'll be remembering that trick next time I see Irby."

"You won't see him, Joe," Yeager said bluntly. "He's dead."

"Dead!" Starting to rear up on his pillows, Joe Hazle grunted and flinched as a streak of pain hit his bandaged ribs, and he sagged back. "Tell me," he ordered harshly.

Yeager gave him the story, all of it. "It was at

the back of my mind I might be able to bring him in for you. More than half-hoping it would be so, I gave him his chance to drop his gun. He wanted no part of that and came up shooting. And, well, that's it, Joe. He's dead."

Sober-faced, Joe Hazle considered before in effect echoing what Lorie Anselm had said earlier. "When I think of it, I see it as one of those things that shape up for a long time and have to be. Just you and him, Hugh. So now it's done with. And damn glad I am it's you who can report it."

"There's another one, Joe," Yeager said grimly. He told of Frenchy Dubois and how and why he died. To this, Joe Hazle's reaction was emphatic and entirely realistic.

"Good riddance! Who'll weep over a damn dry-gulcher? What rifle was he carrying?"

"Winchester .38-56."

"Of course!" Hazle exclaimed. "Ben Hardisty's gun. Which puts that record straight. Two of a kind, Fletch Irby and Frenchy Dubois — now out of the picture for good. Things are clearing up, Hugh."

"Not entirely," Yeager differed. He told of the expected rustling raid. "What's to do about that?"

Joe Hazle groaned his disgust. "And me laid up, useless. I can only give you this word. Bust up the raid, Hugh. Do it any way you have to. Long as Jack Cardinal and his crowd laid quiet on their side of the hills, Haley Lockyear's been willing to leave things so. But it seems once a cow thief, always a cow thief — and the breed never learns except the mean way. Hugh, you hit that gang as hard as you have to and any way you have to!"

Crossing the flats beyond town to the Sheridan Bench range, Yeager considered the word and made his bleak decision.

XII

The Sheridan Bench range never appeared more secure and rewarding. Warm quiet filled the shadows in the timber and in the open areas cattle grazed peacefully or lay resting in the sun, the red and white of their hides strong color against the green of these upland meadows. Here a couple of knobby-legged calves romping at play, broke off butting baby heads to stare round-eyed as Yeager rode by. He wondered at the contrast of such surroundings against the dark and deadly violence that had erupted in the early dawn light at the lower ranch. Wondered too at what lay ahead and how he would manage when he faced it.

On the trail short of headquarters he met Miles Grayson, who showed him an expression and a tone of voice very close to harsh and outright anger.

"Damn you, Hugh! Don't ever do this sort of thing to me and the rest of the crew again. You put us through one hell of a night, waiting and wondering." Then Grayson's true relief came through to break up the hard mask. "So you were faster than Irby?"

"Maybe not faster, but straighter," Yeager

told him, made humble by the honest concern behind Grayson's rough greeting. "From now on, Miles, you'll ride with me."

"Me, and all the others," declared Grayson bluntly. "You'll hear about that from Sam Carlock. I don't know what you got ahead for tonight, but Sam and me and the other boys know what we're going to do, and you better believe we damn well mean it. Now let's get along so the others can shed their worries."

They gathered in the ranch house and old Sam Carlock, flour sack apron tied about his gaunt middle, faced Yeager.

"All right, Hugh," he growled. "Tell it!"

Yeager made it brief and curt. When he finished, Sam Carlock was equally curt.

"So that part's finished and maybe you were lucky. But there'll be no more of this 'one man against the world' foolishness. Oh, we know you meant it well, out of concern for us. But how the hell do you suppose we feel? Say it was you instead of Fletch Irby layin' dead at the lower ranch — think we'd hide out and let the wild ones take over? Like hell we would! So, whatever's ahead we are in it, plumb up to our necks. We're not infants, Hugh — we're men! Treat us as such!"

Yeager's glance touched them all with a grave smile. "Very well. If that's the way you want it, that's the way it will be. We're riding tonight."

"That's better," Carlock approved. "Unless we get Jack Cardinal on the hip and bust him

194

complete, this cow stealin' will go on and on until we're bled white, and some of us, likely enough, will be six feet under. Miles and me, we squeezed some more talk out of Bruno Orr, and what Cardinal's got lined up for us is just as bad as anything Fletch Irby ever thought of. So this better be a deal where we throw all the rules out the window and clean up once and for all, right down to the ground."

"We'll be outnumbered, of course," Yeager reminded. "You've thought of that?"

"All the way," old Sam said. "But there's enough of us if we pick the right time and place and hit them when they least expect it. I been through things like this before, so I know the value of surprise. It can double what you got. And the right place is the badlands of Massacre Pass. Some of those wild ones, none too smart to begin with, are already spooky about that region knowin' what happened there once before."

Yeager yawned and stretched mightily. "That's how it will be then. Last night apparently was a long one for all of us. Tonight can be another like it, so maybe we all better get a little rest."

Grim and purposeful, they left the ranch in the waning afternoon. Bruno Orr rode with them, ankles tied to the cinch rings of his saddle, hands tied to the horn of it.

"You're a small part of nothin', Orr," warned Sam Carlock. "You'll be considerable less than that should you go raunchy on me and stir up trouble. Your best chance of livin' free to ride out of the country when this deal is over is keep your mouth shut and do as you're told."

Sam had the big buffalo Sharps gun across his saddle, and the pockets of his worn and faded jeans were stuffed with the heavy, lethal cartridges. His warning got no argument from Bruno Orr, who had long since decided that what he might owe Jack Cardinal was nothing compared to what he owed himself, so he was fully prepared to speak and act accordingly. Cardinal, he stated flatly, wouldn't come over the pass until the moon was up. And he was to meet him there.

"Not you this time," Sam growled. "But all of us!"

They measured the distance and they measured their pace accordingly. They were climbing the Massacre Pass Road as the sun went down, and dust swelled to cloak the land in a flood of smoky purple. Darkness was full and the sky awash with stars when they topped out on the chill summit, and in the east the sky was turning pallid under the approach of the moon. Scouting carefully ahead, Miles Grayson eased back to report all clear.

They left their horses group-tied below a protective rim with Bruno Orr's mount hobbled as well as tied with the rest.

"You'll be safe enough, providing you cause no trouble," reminded Sam Carlock. "But should you raise a warning yell, then you'll swing from the highest and nearest tree. That's a promise, Orr."

"I ain't a complete damn fool," grumbled Orr. "I'm just hopin' there'll be somebody left to turn me loose when it's over."

They ranged along the road among the rock rims and pinnacles, three on each side, Yeager and Miles Grayson furthest ahead. Like a prowling old panther, Sam Carlock made a last circle, dropping final words of advice.

"You got any noble ideas about giving Cardinal and his crowd a chance — get rid of them. This ain't no friendly waltz, this is war, and war ain't never pretty. It's them or us — cold turkey! So keep low and pick your targets against the stars or the moon. Good luck!"

He had a special word for Johnny Richert, the youngest of the crew, laying a hand on the boy's shoulder.

"You find it hard to pull a trigger, son, don't let it bother you. I'll be handy to take over your share."

While he waited, something like the bitterness of bile gathered at the base of Hugh Yeager's tongue. It wasn't fear, for he'd disposed of all that sort of thing when he faced Fletch Irby in the early dawn. More than anything else, perhaps, it was revulsion. Why, he wondered dismally, did it always have to be this way? Why were there always some who chose the trail of the outlaw when the risks were so great and so many and the rewards so often something less than meager?

Because their way always ended as this would end, with guns rapping out wicked challenge and men dying violently. Still it was one of the oldest of all predicted endings worked out by men in one form or another down through the ages. And always for the same sordid reason — always for gain of some sort; one fighting to maintain a possession, the other fighting to take it away. Maybe, when you stripped it down to the bare bones of fact, it was merely the law of the jungle. . . .

He shook himself to shed the somber burden of such thoughts. Old Sam Carlock had the right slant on this sort of business — as did Joe Hazle. Do what you had to do and think about it later after the first bruises healed.

He reared up a little for a look around. This was hostile country, right enough, this scoured out stretch of gaunt, twisted rock rims and pinnacles. Though the moon was still below the far rim of the world, its approaching reflection was spreading, and if a man let his imagination run, it was not hard, as the luckless Ed Cruze had claimed, to people the night with the flitting phantoms and elusive ghosts of those who had died here in the bloody affair that had named the pass. One of the stars overhead curved across the heavens in a thin streak of dissolving light before burning out in a last pale flare and vanishing into infinity. There was, it seemed, an end to all things — even among the stars. . . .

Abruptly a curved slice of moon lifted above the horizon. Quickly it climbed, swelling into shape even as he watched. Then it was a great, luminous globe, and in the full glow of its white light, what had been dark and shapeless before now became full-formed, edged with a brittle silver. Yeager hunkered back to wait and to listen.

Here was a great and cold silence. The moon seemed to float on a sea of it, and even the faintest stir of air seeping across the summit made its tiny whisper. But now, from below the east approach to the pass, came the first echo of really solid sound, the thump of hoofs along the road. Steadily the sound grew to become a miscellany of hoof echoes, the metallic jingle of bridle chains, the sudden chuffering of a horse, the low-toned voices of men.

Presently, in the moon's light they were visible, a short solid column of riders advancing at a swinging walk, with two of the group side by side and a little ahead of the others. One of that pair — a high, gaunt figure — Yeager knew was Jack Cardinal, and it would have been a simple thing to have laid a gun on him and cut him from his saddle. But Yeager found it was a thing he couldn't do. Someone like Frenchy Dubois would not have hesitated, but he knew a dismaying sense of complete futility. After all the preparation and with so much at stake, was he about to let the entire column ride by unscathed . . . ? How could he start things?

A horse of one of the rustlers answered this for him. In the slow drift of cold air it caught the scent of one of the hidden group beside the road. It snorted, shied, broke up the column in startled confusion. Its rider, instantly alert, fought the animal with tightened reins as he drew a gun and called quick warning.

"Heads up, Jack, heads up! Something wrong here. Watch it!"

After that, Sam Carlock really set things off. His high, shrill yell was a taunt and a challenge and a threat, and it brought a hard ripple of gunfire from the rustler group.

Old Sam yelled again and the big buffalo gun laid down its heavy roar. After that it was quickly a general thing that drew Yeager in.

Out on the road a horse went down in a wild flailing, with others whirling and trampling and rearing in a confused tangle. Gunfire was a steady spreading racket, spikes of gunflame pale in the moon glow. A slug, striking rock only inches from Yeager's head, wailed away in howling ricochet, leaving behind the hot, metallic breath of impact and friction.

A rider, high and gaunt in his saddle, fighting a rearing, terrified mount, spun off the road nearly on top of Yeager. Yeager threw a shot and missed and then the rider drove a shot almost straight down and Yeager felt the burn of the slug across the flat of his shoulders. The rider fought his horse back into the clear as Yeager snapped another shot and knew he'd missed again. But on his third try, he saw that tall, gaunt rider buckle and bend and fall forward along the neck of his horse.

It was a wild, savage business there in the silver glow of the moon with gun echoes rolling and rolling. The hard, ringing crash of rifles, the shorter thudding of revolver fire, and at intervals the deep, rolling boom of Sam Carlock's buffalo gun. It was too fierce to last — something had to give, and did. Horses were down in the road and others, their riders low-crouched and spurring hard, raced back the way they had come. One riderless mount fled after them. And now the gunfire frittered out and a stunned silence returned.

Yeager lifted guarded call and Miles Grayson sent gruff reply.

"All right here. And you . . . ?"

"Singed a little but still lucky. Let's take a look."

There were two horses down in the road, and three smaller, huddled shadows. Miles Grayson scratched a match over one of these and reported. "Mack Snell, this one."

Recalling how such a figure had slumped to his shot, Yeager needed no match to identify the long, sprawled form of Jack Cardinal. And now, from further along, Abe Lancaster called anxiously.

"Hugh — get over here, Hugh!"

Abe and his brother Danny and young Johnny Richert were in a little group about someone

201

flattened beside the road.

"Who is it?" Yeager rapped. "Not — Sam . . . ?"

Sam Carlock answered for himself, his voice thin and drained and tired.

"Told everybody else to stay down, stay low, and then didn't have sense enough — to do it myself. Had to take a final look — and their last shot — got me. Just a damned old fool. . . ."

Yeager was on his knees. "Where, Sam — where?"

"Center, boy — plumb center — by the feel of it. . . . Only — ain't much feelin' left . . . !"

"Hang on, Sam, hang on," Yeager urged. "We'll get you to the ranch — and there's a doctor in town. Hang on!"

"No use, boy," Sam murmured. "I'm headin' a different direction from the ranch — and it's just as well. More useful way to go than cluttering' up a bunk. . . . And who knows — mebbe I'll be meetin' up with Buck Abbott again. You tell Miss Lorie that — should she shed a tear — for old Sam . . ."

That was the all of it; there wasn't any more. And they all understood when young Johnny Richert stumbled away blindly, shoulders hunched and shaking.

They put old Sam across his saddle. "Take him back to the ranch," Yeager told Johnny Richert and the Lancaster boys. "Take Orr along too, and hold him there until Miles and I show up. This has been a rough, dirty business and there's still one more loose end to tie up. Miles and I can handle it."

He listened to the sound of the others moving off into the night. Then he and Miles Grayson moved warily in on Elkhorn Flat, staying with the road only as far as the timber, then using its cover the rest of the way. They rode with some care but no great worries, for the men who had fled the fight in the pass would not be stopping at the flat.

They scouted the edges of things to make sure of this, testing the night again and again and coming up with nothing but silence and emptiness. There was one small light in Gabe Norton's place, but that was all.

They moved in on the deadfall, went in with drawn and ready guns and found Gabe Norton, massive and gross, sitting alone with a bottle and glass. His heavy-lidded eyes barely flickered at their entrance.

"Kind of expected something like this," he said in his thick, moist voice. "You can put away your guns. Everybody's gone — even the woman. Seen it happen before. While the wind's fair and easy, they hang around. But when the ride gets rough . . ." He shrugged. "They went through here, full out. If Cardinal or Snell had been with them, they might have stopped. So . . . ?"

"Cardinal and Snell are back up in the pass, Gabe," Yeager said. "And a third one — a stranger to Miles and me. They'll steal no more cattle."

Norton's big, flaccid-cheeked head nodded slowly. "Something's happened to Fletch Irby, too, or you wouldn't be here. He's dead."

"That's right."

Again Norton nodded, his head bobbing up and down as though he was working a laborious way through heavy, brooding thought. "Man born a fool generally dies a fool," he said at last. "There's a balance in this world no man can beat. I should have thought of that before. So — what's for me?"

His head lifted as he spoke, his little, lead-colored eyes fixed on Yeager's face.

"You're leaving, Gabe," Yeager told him. "I don't know where to, but it better be far off. Because after the first storm hits, I'm burning this layout."

"Destroy the nest, the rats will stay gone. That it?"

"Something like that. You were just too damn friendly with the wrong people, Gabe. I haven't enjoyed this deal. It's been rough and mean and dirty. But having gone this far, I intend to finish it. Yeah, Gabe — you're traveling."

Gabe Norton shrugged his great, fat-padded shoulders. "Long as I have to, reckon I can. Guess I'm lucky, at that. It's like I said — there's a balance no man can beat. I'll be remembering that while I travel."

They buried Sam Carlock at the foot of the hawks-nest pine tree, and after it was done,

Yeager turned Bruno Orr loose.

"A long ride for you too, Bruno."

"That's it," Orr agreed. "A real long one. And alone."

Still later, Yeager headed for town. He felt old and beat and weary as hell, knowing now that even the winner always leaves a lot of himself along any trail of violence.

His first stop was the bank where he gave Frank Cornelius the entire word. Noting the harsh, tired lines of Yeager's face and his deep, burned, sleep-starved eyes, Cornelius murmured, "Man — man — you need some rest . . . !"

Yeager's laugh was a croak. "Rest? What's that? It will come."

He headed for the hotel and Frank Cornelius, watching, nodded. "If Buck Abbott could hear me, I'd tell him he put his money on the right man!"

They were making pies in the hotel kitchen, Helen Stent and Lorie Anselm. At Yeager's step Lorie turned, stared and then came quickly to him, wiping flour-whitened hands on her red and white checked apron. Marking the same look Frank Cornelius had, she swung a chair around exclaiming her concern.

"Hugh — Hugh — you're dead on your feet!"

He slacked into the chair, sighing deeply, letting his shoulders sag. "Pretty soon," he said woodenly. "I'm going to sleep for a week. But first — you got to know, Lorie. Sam Carlock is gone. He was killed last night when we busted up Jack Cardinal and his rustling crew. We buried Sam under the hawks-nest tree at the upper ranch. You were on his mind when he died."

Again the resolution and strength of this slim girl surprised him. "I'll weep for Sam when I tend his grave," she said steadily. "But right now it's the hurt I see in you that concerns me. Is it over, Hugh — all of it?"

"All of it," he nodded. "You can go back to your ranch, Lorie."

She did what she had done before. She took his head in her arms and held it close, and Yeager knew that here was a warm, sure comfort that would never end.

The employees of G.K. Hall hope you have enjoyed this Large Print book. All our Large Print titles are designed for easy reading, and all our books are made to last. Other G.K. Hall books are available at your library, through selected book-stores, or directly from us.

For information about titles, please call:

(800) 257-5157

To share your comments, please write:

Publisher
G.K. Hall & Co.
P.O. Box 159
Thorndike, ME 04986